JP

✓

Withdrawn

A HANDFUL OF MIST

When Deborah was widowed she didn't particularly want to sell her house, but if she was to earn a living for herself and her small daughter she didn't see any alternative — until Mark Nesbit, also widowed, wanted a home for his two teenage children. He offered to buy her house on condition that she stayed on as housekeeper for a year. Deborah was soon wishing it was for a lifetime, but would Mark ever see her as anything but a housekeeper?

JANE CARRICK

A HANDFUL
OF MIST

Complete and Unabridged

LINFORD
Leicester

First published in Great Britain in 1973
under the name of
'Mary Cummins'

First Linford Edition
published 2001

All the characters in this book have no existence
outside the imagination of the Author, and
have no relation whatsoever to anyone
bearing the same name or names. They are
not even distantly inspired by any individual
known or unknown to the Author, and all the
incidents are pure invention.

British Library CIP Data

Carrick, Jane
    A handful of mist.—Large print ed.—
Linford romance library
1. Love stories
2. Large type books
I. Title II. Cummins, Mary
823.9'14 [F]

ISBN 0–7089–5931–8

Published by
F. A. Thorpe (Publishing)
Anstey, Leicestershire

Set by Words & Graphics Ltd.
Anstey, Leicestershire
Printed and bound in Great Britain by
T. J. International Ltd., Padstow, Cornwall

This book is printed on acid-free paper

1

Mark Nesbit hardly knew why he had chosen the Isle of Man, unless it was a strange quirk of fate which had made him glance down the advertisement column of a national newspaper.

The house which was for sale seemed to leap at him from the pages, and he read the advertisement, then read it again. The house was spacious and sounded attractive, though past experience had taught him that it would bear investigation. He had put the paper aside while he attended to his business affairs in Manchester, then later as he had relaxed in his room at the Midland Hotel, he got it out again and stared at the advertisement thoughtfully. He could fly over from Blackpool tomorrow, and delay his return to Glasgow by one more day. The house might be completely unsuitable, but a quick look would settle the matter.

At the moment, thoughts of it kept intruding into urgent business matters and he would have no clear-cut details to discuss with Robert McLean, his partner in an engineering business, when he returned to the office on Monday.

Yet it was essential that he found a house soon, for Rory's sake . . . somewhere quiet where the boy could come to terms with himself again. Rory had wanted somewhere miles from civilisation as they knew it, in the north of Scotland perhaps, or one of the Western Isles. But Frances wanted to go with him, and surely a girl of her age didn't want to be cut off all that much from the world she knew, for an indefinite period of time.

Mark Nesbit had rung up the airport the following morning and learned that there would be a flight to suit him. Having made up his mind, he was quick to act upon it, and now here he was, in a small aircraft, approaching Ronaldsway Airport, and looking down on the island he had not seen or even thought about very much in almost thirty years.

He had been very young then ... little older than Rory now ... but he still remembered the hotels on the sea front at Douglas which had been given over to Army occupation. Others, less happily, had been for the internment of prisoners of war.

He also remembered other things about the beautiful island which he and Una had learned to love, even as they had loved one another. She, too, had been young, looking fair and delicate in her heavy khaki uniform, but for four happy months they had spent every available moment together, walking hand in hand along the sands, watching the sea lash against the rocks, roaming over the Island, and gazing at the colourful shops in Douglas, not yet dulled by wartime austerity.

Places like Derby Castle and the Villa Marina were only vaguely remembered, yet once they had been the centre of his world.

Mark Nesbit's eyes were suddenly bleak as he remembered, and for a wild moment he wished he hadn't come aboard this plane. It was a mistake to bring Rory here, and Frances. Then he remembered that the bitter-sweet memories were all his, and that he would only be coming on visits, even if he did move them here. He would have to find a housekeeper who would keep an eye on them. There would have to be changes, anyway, now that Mrs Cleland, their present housekeeper, wanted to go and live with her daughter, and could only come in daily.

Mark collected his scattered thoughts as the plane touched down on the runway. He would look at the house, then make his decision.

But suppose that decision didn't suit Rory . . . or Frances? Shouldn't he consult them first of all? Almost impatiently he collected his belongings. Too much time had already been wasted shilly-shallying. The decisions must come from him.

* * *

Deborah Lacey put down the telephone and glanced anxiously over the sitting-room before tidying up magazines and newspapers, and plumping up cushions. Few would-be buyers had called in answer to her advertisements, but at least she had been spared the curiosity-seekers, and the dreamers with nothing practical behind the dreams.

For a moment she gazed out of the wide low windows at the familiar view of grassy slopes leading down to a lovely bay, with the wide vista of sea beyond. On a clear day she could see the Cumberland coast, visualising the small town of Silloth where she had been born.

When she and Patrick had married, and he had brought her to live on the island which meant so much to him, she had kept the feeling of loneliness and the fact that she was cut off by the sea from the mainland, all to herself. Patrick's home was beautiful, yet it

5

seemed as though it still belonged to the Laceys, even though she had never known Patrick's parents. They had both died years before he met Deborah.

'Mother would have loved you, darling,' Patrick often told her, as he saw her arranging flowers in the kitchen and carrying them into the lovely bright sitting-room.

Deborah had made few changes to Rock House, especially after Amy was born six years ago. Patrick was a solicitor in Douglas and travelled daily, and Deborah had plenty to do in looking after her baby and entertaining Patrick's friends to worry about whether or not she liked Rock House. She had made friends of her own and gradually she began to admire the view from the sitting-room window for its own sake, and not with longing.

But now Patrick, too, had died after a short illness, and Deborah was left, stunned with shock, and Amy dependent on her. He had been older than she, a quiet man with a scholarly appearance and a thin delicate body. He had been unable to throw off the fever which had affected him.

Deborah had consulted John Carlie, Patrick's partner, and after her position became clear, realised that she would have to sell Rock House.

'I'll go back to the mainland,' she informed John Carlie, 'and get a job at teaching again. Perhaps I can keep Amy with me that way. She's too young yet for boarding school.'

'Anything I can do to help, Deb,' said John rather awkwardly, ' . . . you know I'll do all I can . . . '

'I ought to be well enough off after I sell Rock House,' Deborah said with a smile. 'It's just that the house is too big to keep up on the income I'm likely to have, and I doubt if I'll find a job here to pay me as much money as I need.'

'Have you any people on the mainland?'

'An aunt in Whitehaven. Some cousins, too. I shan't be entirely alone.'

'That's good,' John told her, relieved.

He and Patrick had been partners for ten years, but the business wasn't really well enough established yet. And now he had his own family to think about.

'I'll advertise, then,' Deborah was saying, 'in one or two of the national newspapers, I think.'

'There I can help you,' said John, relieved, but glad to be of some assistance. 'If you're determined to sell.'

'I have no choice,' said Deborah quietly.

Yet over the past day or two, something had been growing in her, and it was with no small dismay that she realised how little she wanted to part with the lovely house, or the island. Amy was a small child of six, delicately boned like her father, and she had never known anything but the sheltering love and security of this old house.

At first Deborah had vaguely realised that telling Amy they would be leaving Rock House, and going from the island, would be a problem, but as the days went on, she began to feel the strength of the roots she, herself, had put down. She loved it all, the sea, the small coves, the grassy slopes, the enchantment of the island folklore, and the love of the people whom she had come to regard as her own.

Yet somehow she must welcome this man who had flown over from Blackpool to look at her home, with a view to making it his. Somehow she must hope that he would buy it and relieve her of the responsibility of keeping it up. Her own future home with Amy must be much smaller, with less to do and more time to spare for the employment she would need to take up. And jobs were so hard to find . . . the sort of ideal job she had in mind . . .

The shrill ringing of the doorbell startled her, and Deborah smoothed her auburn hair nervously before walking to the door.

A tall man stood on the step, his body thin but without Patrick's frailty, his dark hair greying a little.

'Mrs Lacey?'

She nodded. 'Yes. Please come in, Mr . . . '

'Nesbit. Mark Nesbit.'

She led the way into the sitting-room, then turned to smile at him, awkwardly, and pull herself together. Now she must do her best to sell Rock House to this completely strange man.

★ ★ ★

Mark Nesbit felt strangely tired as he stood in the sitting-room and tried to smile politely at the owner of the house, a slim young woman who hardly looked more than a girl. She had long auburn hair drawn back into coils at the back of her head, her face lightly powdered with freckles.

She surveyed him coolly, giving him a firm handshake, then set about showing him the house in a brisk, businesslike manner. He had no eyes to see that the house was comfortable, but not ostentatious, that it had been beautifully kept but hardly canonised, merely nodding while she pointed out certain improvements to the old structure and other repairs which could do with attention.

'My . . . my husband had that in mind,' she told him, pointing out a small damp patch above a window. 'I think the guttering needs a small repair.'

There were five bedrooms and three rooms downstairs, with a large kitchen and utility room. The sitting-room was the one which attracted Mark, running the length of the house with a large bay window seat. Here one could sit and watch the changing moods of the sea, and here one could dream a little . . . or perhaps find oneself . . .

He thought of Rory. Couldn't the boy be happy here? But what of the loneliness? And Frances? Who would look after them? Their present house-keeper would not be willing to leave Glasgow and settle down on this island. She was a city woman and needed the heartbeat of the big city as she needed her own, and besides, he still needed her in Glasgow.

'Perhaps you ought to bring your wife,' Mrs Lacey was saying coolly.

He came out of his thoughts, startled.

'I . . . I beg your pardon.'

'Your wife,' she repeated, and he saw that she was looking at him levelly. 'There's a great deal in a house which only concerns the woman who takes care of it. I must be frank, Mr Nesbit. I don't want to sell my home, but I have no alternative, and I don't want to mess about over the sale. I would much rather hear that it's unsuitable than that you change your mind later. I know you'll want to think about it, but . . . but I can't promise to keep the house for anyone . . . '

Her voice trailed off. It was almost as though he had not heard a word she was saying.

'Is there a hotel on the island where I could stay?'

She almost laughed.

'Oh, Mr Nesbit, there are . . . '

'I mean nearby.'

She considered.

'I know somewhere, yes.'

'I'll stay overnight. It will mean a change of plan. May I come and see you again tomorrow, then I promise you I shall give you a decision, one way or another.'

She nodded, her eyes uncertain.

'Very well. But . . . '

'I have no wife,' he said quietly, 'but I have a son and daughter. My wife died . . . two years ago.'

'I see.' She looked at him awkwardly, her own grief and loneliness never far from the surface. 'I . . . I know how you feel.'

'Do you?' he asked harshly, and she felt rebuffed, the warm colour darkening her skin.

'I'll get you that address,' she said quietly, and again he nodded.

He stood in the bay window looking out at the view, his hands in his pockets, while she wrote down instructions. She

felt angry and upset, yet a vague compassion stirred in her as she looked over
at his tall spare figure. He looked lonely,
and alone. Yet he was not alone. He had
his son and daughter, even as she, too,
had her daughter. Neither of them were
alone.

'Would . . . would you care for some
tea?' she offered diffidently.

'Thank you, no. Perhaps tomorrow, if
the offer is still open.'

She said nothing. She would see what
tomorrow would bring.

'Au revoir then, Mrs Lacey,' he said,
smiling suddenly so that she felt taken
aback.

'I . . . I hope you'll be comfortable at
the address I've given you,' she said,
and he shrugged. He thought little of
comfort when it was only one night.
'Though I'm sure you will,' she added,
then felt she was fussing.

This man made her feel very unsure
of herself, though she saw him to the
door, pointing out the direction he
must take to the hotel she had

recommended, then she went back indoors, glad that it was time to go and collect Amy who was at a friend's birthday party, and glad, too, of Amy's childish, excited chatter as they walked home together.

Amy was happy as a sprite. There were no shadows in her life as she ran on her small slender legs, like a young deer dewy-soft with youth. Yet soon the shadows must lengthen, and Deborah Lacey felt the sudden chill in the breeze blowing up from the sea. Soon they would no longer be within the shelter of Rock House. If only Amy would remain unaffected by the change!

2

Mark Nesbit returned to Rock House shortly after ten the following morning. He still looked tired, but his smile was warm and relaxed when Deborah opened the door in response to his ring. Amy was playing with her dolls when he was shown into the sitting-room, and she looked up at him, smiling shyly.

Mark stopped for a moment.

'I didn't know you had a child.'

'Yes.' She hesitated, her eyes growing cool.

'This is Amy. Does it matter?'

He stared at Amy, then smiled again.

'Hello, Amy.' He walked forward and knelt down in a friendly way. 'Won't you introduce me to that pretty dolly?'

'She's called Pat,' said Amy shyly.

'Pat? For Patricia, no doubt,' he said, rising to stand, again, beside Deborah.

'No. For Pat. Pending . . . on the

16

back of the doll's neck. Amy was learning to read at the time.'

'Surely she's very young to be reading?'

'She's six. She's been reading since she was four. Her . . . her father was a scholarly man and I think Amy will take after him.'

Deborah stopped. Why should she tell all this to Mark Nesbit? And what concern could it be of his whether she had a daughter or not?

'Won't it upset the child . . . changing schools as well as a new home?' he was asking.

'It will be my concern to see that she is upset as little as possible,' said Deborah stiffly. 'Now, Mr Nesbit, about the house . . . '

He was still staring thoughtfully at the child, stroking his upper lip as though it had once sprouted a moustache which was no longer there.

'Oh. Oh, yes . . . I'm sorry, Mrs Lacey, I . . . I was thinking, I'm afraid. A bad habit of mine. May I sit down?'

17

'Of course.' She was confused, feeling that she had been ungracious. 'May I get you some coffee? There's some ready now.'

'The aroma is delicious,' he said, smiling again. 'I would welcome a cup.'

When she returned from the kitchen, he helped her with the tray, pushing forward a small coffee table. For Amy there was orange juice and a biscuit, with a tiny one on a doll's plate for Pat.

'I would like to bring my son here to live,' said Mark abruptly.

Deborah smiled.

'If you buy the house, then I hope you, and your family, will be happy here . . . '

'No please, let me tell you about it a little. I have a problem, you see, and I can't give you a definite answer till that problem is solved. At the moment my son and daughter are living in the family home, on the outskirts of Glasgow. It was my parents' home, then it came to me when they died. My wife

18

and I lived there, and our children were born there.

'When . . . when my wife died two years ago . . . in a car accident . . . my sister came to live with us and look after the children. At first it was only Frances who was then attending High School, then later it was Rory, too.'

'Had he been away at school?'

'No. No, he'd been in hospital. He . . . was in the car, you see. His face was cut, and there was a burn which has had to heal. Later there was plastic surgery, but Rory . . . he hates to be so near his friends till his face isn't so disfigured. At first they kept coming, but he grew sensitive. He felt they were giving him pity, but he . . . well, he's imagining too much, Mrs Lacey. His friends accept the scars, I'm sure. But they go deep, like the roots of weeds.'

He was silent, and she hardly knew what to say. She could offer this man her pity, but he wouldn't want that. Instead she quietly took his coffee cup and refilled it, handing it to him.

'And like weeds, they can be erased,' he told her, almost vehemently, 'but Rory must have patience. He's . . . he's becoming difficult, Mrs Lacey. He wants to get away, almost hide himself away from people, friends, everything.'

'He would meet people here,' said Deborah.

'Strangers, yes. Strangers who would accept him as he is *now*. It would be better for him than not meeting anyone, as he wants it to be.'

'Then . . . then he doesn't really want to come here?'

'He knows nothing about it. He wanted a cottage in the Highlands somewhere, a remote place away from our type of civilisation. I think this house would be better for him. It would help him to come to terms with himself . . . heal the scars underneath, so that when his face is better, he'll be a whole man again.'

Deborah put down her cup carefully.

'But . . . but you can't just make him come here. He might hate it. You'd have to give him some sort of say in what he wants.'

For the first time she noticed the firming of Mark Nesbit's mouth. He was the sort of man who would be difficult to move once he had made up his mind.

'Rory changes his mind over what he wants every five minutes,' he told her. 'He's just got through his 'A' levels in three subjects, after private tuition. When his medical treatment is finished, he will apply for entrance to university. In the meantime he writes a little.'

'Writes? You mean for his own amusement? As a hobby?'

Again Mark smiled.

'Not Rory! No, he writes articles and stories, some of which he sells.'

'He sounds an interesting boy, Mr Nesbit.'

She was silent for a while, idly watching Amy industriously changing the clothing on her doll, which was being prepared for bed.

'If you feel your son would be happy

here, then I hope he will . . . '

'It isn't as simple as that.' Mark Nesbit rose abruptly, and paced the floor, his dark brown shoes brilliant with polish. 'My sister came to stay with us two years ago when her daughter left home and married. Marion was widowed when she was young . . . like you. She brought up her son single-handed, and made a fine job of it.'

Mark's eyes rested gently on Amy.

'Now she's getting married again,' he said, with a smile.

'Oh.'

Deborah began to see his predicament. 'And your daughter is too young to take on the responsibility? Didn't you say you had a housekeeper, though?'

'She certainly won't leave Glasgow! Besides, I shall want to keep on my home there, and I need her to look after it. But Frances insists on going with Rory. She's only eighteen, and Rory is almost twenty . . . too young to be on their own.'

'And you?'

'I shall have to stay in Glasgow. My business is there,' he said, briskly. 'I'm in engineering. I would only be able to come for a long weekend, perhaps once a month . . . oftener if I can manage it.'

She frowned. 'Then surely a house nearer your present home would be more suitable . . . ' He didn't answer, and she said gently, 'No, I can see it wouldn't. I'm sorry.'

He turned on his heel.

'Are your plans already made, Mrs Lacey? Wouldn't you consider staying on here, just to keep an eye on Rory and Frances? I . . . I would be willing to pay you any salary you care to name . . . within reason, of course. I . . . '

She was astounded, staring at him blankly, so that he flushed darkly.

'No, I can see you wouldn't. It was impertinent of me to suggest it. I apologise. It was just that . . . well, it might have been a good solution for both of us. You could still live in your own home, though, of course, without the financial responsibility of its upkeep. Your daughter would not be upset. She could still attend her local school and you . . . '

'But it wouldn't be my home!' she cried. 'Not any longer. It would be yours! I should have to stay on here, knowing that it all belonged to someone else.'

He nodded.

'It will belong to someone else in any case, if you decide to sell.'

'I have to sell it,' she said, in a low voice. 'There are . . . er . . . expenses which must be met. That's why I'm selling the house as it stands.'

For a long time they were both silent. Deborah found she couldn't lightly dismiss the proposition which Mark Nesbit had put to her. She would hate such a thing, she told herself, seeing a strange boy and girl in her home which would no longer be her home. Even with help in the house, she would have a great deal more to do.

Yet there was Amy. How wonderful it

would be if Amy didn't have to be upset.

'Oh well,' said Mark, with a sigh as he turned to her, 'I suppose it was worth a try. I shall have to be sure of a housekeeper, though, before I make a definite offer for the house. You understand?'

'Yes.' She nodded. Her eyes were troubled as she looked at him.

'Shall we both take a week to think it over?'

'A week ... yes ... perhaps that would be best.'

He held out his hand.

'Shall we shake on it, in case neither of us feel like shaking hands later?'

She put out a small slender hand, and as he took it, his smile grew uncertain. He was beginning to notice that she was delicately built.

'Perhaps I was asking too much of you anyway,' he remarked. 'Rory isn't the easiest of mortals at the moment, though I only intended that you run the home for him and Frances. It's she who

25

would be responsible for cheering him up.'

'Isn't she rather young for such responsibility, too?' Deborah asked rather gently.

'The decision was hers,' said Mark in a way which shut the door to discussion.

He walked towards the door and she came to see him out, but before leaving he turned to her again.

'This is a happy house. Has it always been so?'

'I expect so. I . . . I haven't really thought about it. Patrick and I were happy and I was very sad and lonely when he died. But he was older than I, and delicate in health. I . . . I suppose I felt all along that some day I might be . . . well, on my own, but for Amy. I do have Amy, you know.'

'I hope I can bring my children here,' he said quietly. 'Our own home has not been happy, since my wife died.'

'You must miss her a great deal,' she said softly.

'Yes. But . . . but there's more to it than that. Something has gone out of our home . . . or crept into it. I don't know which. I shall be glad to move Rory and Frances somewhere else.'

But home isn't just a house, thought Deborah, as she shut the door after he had left. Home is built up of the people living in it, and their love for one another. Perhaps Rory and Frances would bring their unhappiness with them if they came here.

She sat down for a moment, looking at Amy. She couldn't do it. But even as she washed up in the kitchen, she knew that she was going to try.

★ ✸ ★

In the week which followed, Deborah felt as though her life swung to and fro like a pendulum. At times the very thought of having strangers in her home, using her things was untenable to her, then it occurred to her that if she let the house, there would still be

27

strangers here, using her things. That thought stuck in her mind, and she wondered if, in fact, it wouldn't be possible to let the house. Perhaps Mark Nesbit would be willing to lease it from her, instead of her having to take the final step of selling it.

But another look at her financial position showed her, sadly, that it wasn't possible. She would only be able to keep the few personal items of furniture, ornaments and small family treasures she had already set aside to keep.

Two days before Mark Nesbit was due to ring for her final decision, she left Amy with a baby-sitter and went into Douglas to spend the evening with John and Margaret Carlie. John had been Patrick's senior partner, and Deborah still relied on him and Margaret for any advice and support.

It was one of their usual cosy evenings round the fire, and for a while Deborah was very silent, thinking how often they had all spent such an

evening, with Patrick sitting on another large easy chair talking contentedly to John while she and Margaret found plenty to say to one another.

Now she felt that the other two were aware of the gap in her life, and felt uncomfortable in the fact that they could do little to help her, but offer sympathy. She came out of her thoughts, and managed to smile at them both.

'Sorry. I'm poor company this evening.'

'That's all right, Debbie. We understand. Don't we, John?'

'Certainly. No need to make polite conversation in this house.'

'Oh, but I do need to . . . I mean, I would like to ask your advice . . . both of you.'

Margaret glanced at John.

'If we can do anything . . . '

'No, nothing like that. Only advice, Margaret.' As briefly as possible she told them about Mr Nesbit's visit, without going into more than the bare necessary facts of private details.

'It would be a solution,' said Deborah, 'especially with Amy to consider. Besides, no one else has answered the advertisement, and no one seems to be falling over themselves to come along and give me even a reasonable offer. The house is too big for a retired couple, and too inconveniently placed for the normal family.'

Margaret's eyes were bright with interest and excitement.

'And you wouldn't have to leave the island! For purely selfish reasons, that would be splendid, Deb.'

But John was pulling at his chin.

'He's asking a bit much,' he decided, 'putting you in charge of a couple of teenage youngsters. Too much responsibility, Deborah.'

'They aren't children,' she pointed out. 'If I find their behaviour difficult, I can soon get in touch with Mr Nesbit. It's really only a temporary measure, too, and maybe it will give me time to make better plans for Amy and me.

Don't forget, I trained as a teacher even if I didn't have a great deal of practical experience before I married Patrick. But it would come in useful in handling Rory and Frances Nesbit. They might be darlings anyway.'

'A boy whose face has been marred, and a girl leaving her own circle of friends to keep her brother company . . . there'll be problems, Deborah.'

'Well, I'm going to tackle them,' she said, almost defiantly, and knew that her mind was now made up.

'Good for you,' Margaret approved. 'It's a challenge, and you like a challenge, darling. I mean, marrying Patrick was a challenge . . . in a way . . . '

Margaret's voice trailed off lamely, as she realised she might have put her foot in it.

Soon Deborah got to her feet, saying she would have to go home early for the sake of her baby-sitter.

'I'll let you know what happens,' she promised Margaret.

'We'll stick by you, whatever happens,' Margaret promised.

'Thank you.'

Deborah left feeling rather more lighthearted. It was good to have friends.

3

Mark Nesbit's telephone call was terse and businesslike. He had now considered things carefully and he would like to make a firm offer for Rock House, plus any furniture which was included in the sale, if Mrs Lacey would consider staying on as housekeeper for at least a year.

A year would pass, thought Deborah. One can put up with anything, if one knows it is only for a limited period.

'Are your son and daughter happy about coming to live here?' she asked, and this time there was hesitation in the firm deep voice.

'They aren't likely to be completely happy about any move at the moment,' Mark Nesbit told her.

Deborah felt she'd had her answer.

'I shall engage other staff to help you, of course, Mrs Lacey. No doubt you already have help in the house?'

'Only Mrs Wilson from Laxey village. Once a week. I could ask her to come more often.'

'As often as you would wish. Is it agreed then, Mrs Lacey?'

'Agreed,' she said firmly.

'A week should be enough to arrange things from this end. That all right with you?'

'Perfectly all right. I shall prepare the bedrooms though if your son and daughter . . . '

'Rory and Frances.'

'Rory and Frances,' she repeated, 'if they wish to make changes, they can do so. I'll move Amy and myself into the small bedroom at the end of the house . . . '

'No,' he said sharply, 'you must keep to your present arrangement. Your bedroom can be a bedsitting-room, if you wish. I shall have the smaller one as I expect only to be a weekend visitor.'

'Very well,' she agreed, then added,

'thank you. You're being very thought-ful.'

'Not at all. If you aren't happy, you won't stay. And I need you to stay.'

She said nothing, and after a few more remarks, he said he would make all the necessary arrangements regarding purchase, and pay her rent till the contract was signed, if that was satisfactory.

Deborah returned to her neglected pot of tea and plate of buttered toast, by the fireside. She had been feeling her own loneliness, and now that her decision was made, she found herself half wishing the week gone. She had been very tired after Patrick's death, but now she found energy returning, and a wish to get on with her life again. Whatever the future brought, it would be a welcome challenge.

'Read me a story, Mummy,' Amy pleaded, climbing on to her knee and presenting her favourite book of Manx fairy tales. 'Read about the Doinney-Oie and the Taroo-Ushtey.'

'All right, darling,' Deborah laughed. 'Amy, we have a young lady and gentleman coming to stay, and this is going to be their house now.'

'Where will our house be?' Amy asked.

'Here. We'll live here, too.'

'Read me that one,' said Amy.

'Do you understand, darling? The house will belong to Rory and Frances.'

'Rory and Frances,' Amy repeated. 'Read that one.'

Deborah sighed and started to read the fairy tale. Amy didn't understand, but surely there would be no complications on that account.

★   ★   ★

The Nesbits had crossed on the car ferry from Ardrossan, and the car was loaded with personal goods and cases as it drew up outside the front entrance. Deborah was there to meet them, and she looked eagerly at the slim, slender girl who stepped out of the car at the same time as her father, then turned to help her brother, equally thin, but tall and dark as a gypsy. As he turned to stare at her, Deborah felt a small intake of breath at the bitter scar which ran down the right side of his face, marring what must have been outstanding good looks.

Her training as a teacher stood her in good stead, however, as she met his gaze with frankness, showing neither pity nor revulsion. She saw him relax a little, as though he had braced himself to face something which was not there after all.

Then Mark was walking forward with his hand on the girl's arm.

'Mrs Lacey! Hello, nice to see you again. This is my daughter, Frances.'

'How do you do,' Deborah smiled, holding out her hand. 'I . . . I hope you'll like your new home and . . . and enjoy staying here.'

Frances met her gaze levelly, but there was no sign of emotion on her face. She had a small delicately boned face with large violet-blue eyes and long shining hair, gypsy black as her brother's. Slender as a wand, Deborah thought she had rarely seen a lovelier girl, yet it was as though the spark of light which could turn her into a sparkling princess of a girl was gone. Deborah couldn't even guess if Frances had come willingly or not.

But there was no doubt about Rory, as he came forward to shake hands, and stare beyond her at his new home. Rory hadn't come in the least willingly, and she could see it in the flashing looks which passed between him and his father.

'I hope you'll be happy here,' Deborah told him lamely, as she shook hands.

'Oh, I'll be fine,' he said, with a small laugh which wasn't exactly a heartening sound. 'Don't worry about me, Mrs Lacey.'

'This is Amy,' said Deborah, as they went into the lounge. 'I hope you don't mind having a small girl around . . .'

For a moment a smile flitted across Frances' face, and even Rory nodded to the child.

'Hello, Amy.'

'Hello, Frances.'

'No, this is Frances, dear. And this is Rory.'

Amy was overcome with shyness at making a mistake and retreated with her toys to a quiet corner of the room.

'Tea will be ready shortly, but if you care to see the bedrooms, and have a wash . . . If you wish to make any changes, of course . . . '

'Of course,' said Rory, but Mark, coming in with another case, was soon getting things organised. Deborah was relieved when he said he intended to stay overnight. At least she had a day's grace before she began the uphill task of getting to know these two young people, and trying to make them happy and comfortable for the next year.

'I'll have to get used to your likes and dislikes,' she said brightly, as she poured tea for them all. 'In the

39

meantime, I've rather played for safety in regard to the food.'

'Mrs Cleland is a very good cook,' Rory told her.

'I'm only passable, I'm afraid,' said Deborah.

Mark Nesbit was strangely silent, though he ate his meal with obvious enjoyment.

'I hope you two will take yourself off for a walk after tea,' he said bluntly. 'It's quiet down there at that cove. I've things I wish to discuss with Mrs Lacey.'

'Oh, they needn't, if they don't wish,' put in Deborah hastily. 'My . . . my husband's old study . . . yours now . . . is quite private.'

'No, we'll go out, Mrs Lacey,' said Frances.

'As Father says, it's quiet down at the cove,' put in Rory.

She refused to notice that he had emphasised the word 'quiet'.

'Very well, just as you like. First of all, I shall show you round, if I may, then you can get your bearings.'

'I'll do that if you like,' Mark offered, and again she hesitated. She would like to have seen the young people's reaction to her home, now theirs. She and Patrick had been rather conservative in their tastes. Would these young people find it all too dull for them? Would they expect something more adventurous in the way of decorations and furnishings? Oh well, that had been up to Mark Nesbit, she reminded herself. It was no longer her affair.

But as she washed up, allowing Amy to dry one or two of her precious best teacups and saucers, she sighed a little. She didn't know what she had expected, but it hadn't been anything better. Nor any worse, she thought wryly.

★ ★ ★

Mark left again for Glasgow early the following day, deciding to fly this time and ringing up for a booking to

Abbotsinch. Later Mrs Wilson arrived to help in the house.

Rory and Frances were already up and wandering around rather aimlessly, while Deborah wondered in what possible way she could encourage them to occupy their time. She had asked Mark before he left, but he seemed rather vague on the subject.

'Oh, Rory will likely have some reading or writing to do, and Frances will amuse herself, I've no doubt.'

'What's she going to do with her life, Mr Nesbit?'

'She'll find something, when Rory is better, I expect.'

'Didn't she want to carry on her studies?'

Mark smiled ruefully.

'Frances didn't particularly like school. She was very persuasive about making me agree to her leaving.'

Only now she was here on Deborah's hands, no doubt soon to be bored. Surely she couldn't devote her whole life to keeping Rory's spirits up! They had both accepted the bedrooms Deborah had selected for them without asking to change, and she felt she might have preferred a fuss. At least that way she would have known they cared!

But now Frances had gone back upstairs, saying she still had a few things to unpack, and Rory mooched around the drawing room, hands in pockets.

'Poor lovey,' whispered Mrs Wilson to Deborah in the kitchen, though her rather gravelly voice could often be heard throughout the house. 'His poor face all bashed at his age!'

Deborah heard his swift movement, and a moment later the front door slammed as he made for the cove. She wondered if she ought to alert Frances to keep an eye on him. Did Rory get black moods? Did he despair at all when he was forcibly reminded of his scars?

She hesitated, then the problem was solved for her as Frances ran lightly downstairs, clad in a swirling pleated dress and dainty shoes. Had she only brought dress-up clothes? wondered Deborah.

'Where's Rory?' she asked.

'Gone to the cove, I should think.'

She, too, made for the door and Deborah began to call her back, then let it go. Frances would soon find out for herself if her clothes were all wrong.

It was May, a capricious month for weather, and although the sun had been warm, its brightness reflected in the sea that early morning, the ready clouds were gathering and a breeze blowing up.

'They won't stay out long,' said Mrs Wilson comfortably. 'We'll have rain soon.'

Even as she spoke, the large wet raindrops slashed the window and ten minutes later Rory and Frances arrived back, wet and dishevelled. The girl's long black hair clung to her face, and her dainty skirt swung limply.

'Is it always like this?' asked Rory.

'Not always,' Deborah smiled. 'You'll

have to get used to the weather.'

'Better get a bath and a change of clothing. Mrs Wilson is making some hot coffee.'

They said nothing, but their silence was worse than angry remarks would have been. It was a poor start, and Deborah would have liked a few words with Mark Nesbit. She had thought the youngsters had come here with indifference or reluctance, but now she could see that they didn't want to be here at all!

They would take time to settle, she consoled herself, as the next few days passed without any appreciable change in the weather. Even Mrs Wilson's unfailing cheerfulness wavered a little, and she lost a great deal of her sympathy for Rory. Then Deborah rebelled.

The following Monday she got up with a headache, and even Amy was peevish as she went off to school. Mrs Wilson had declared that she could, after all, only come twice a week and hoped Mrs Lacey would understand.

Mrs Lacey understood. It was a big house and the two young people made a great deal of extra work.

When Rory and Frances appeared late for breakfast, she faced them squarely.

'All right, you two. Let's lay our cards on the table. If this . . . this experiment is to work, then you'll have to stop behaving like spoilt, sulky children. You, Rory, if you have something to study, or to write if you wish, can disappear into the small study immediately after breakfast and get down to some work. And you, Frances, can help me to tidy the bedrooms . . . '

'We didn't ask to come here!' cried Frances. 'It was Daddy . . . '

'That doesn't concern me,' cut in Deborah. 'I didn't particularly want to stay on here as a housekeeper either, but life has a habit of handing out some unpalatable food sometimes. Either we try to make a go of it, or you go back home, and we forget the whole thing. I can always make other arrangements. But if you stay here, you both stop loafing.'

They stared back at her.

'What point is there in work?' asked Rory. 'My last batch of stories and articles all came back.'

Deborah boiled.

'Oh, for goodness' sake, stop feeling so sorry for yourself!' she cried. 'You're a big strong boy . . . or you will be after a few weeks here . . . and that scar on your face will soon be a mere mark of interest, if it shows at all. You've got a good brain or you wouldn't have such good 'A' levels, and you *have* sold *some* of your writing. What are you interested in at the moment?'

'Law,' he told her sullenly.

'My husband was a solicitor . . . '

'Manx law?'

She ignored that.

'He has books in there in plenty, so I expect you to get on with it, as he did. When you tire of reading, you can help out in the garden. At this time of year, it needs all the help it can get.'

'I can help in the garden,' said Frances, and Deborah wondered if the sudden offer was born out of a liking for gardening, or to take her off Rory's back.

'After you help with the beds. You never even make your own.'

'Surely that Mrs Wilson . . . '

'Is only coming twice a week, and shouldn't be expected to make yours anyway.'

Rory rose to his feet.

'All right, if that's how it's got to be. We don't like being here, but it may as well be here as anywhere.'

Deborah said nothing, feeling that she had used up her energy, as Rory walked out of the kitchen. She turned to the young girl.

'As soon as you're ready, Frances, we'll wash up.' Then she saw the worry in her eyes. 'Don't be upset. Rory needs to have something to do.'

'What do you know about Rory? Or me either?' Frances asked, staring her straight in the face, and Deborah had a sense of shock. There was a wealth of sadness and pity in the girl's eyes, far more than she would have expected under the circumstances.

'Why . . . '

'There's no self-pity in Rory. Or me either, for that matter. We'll do what you want, but don't think you've got us all measured up, taped, and the old, old cure of hard work to pull out of your pocket.'

Deborah felt shaken. It was becoming obvious that the problem of these children went deeper than she had supposed, and that a few months on an island for general health to be built up was not likely to be enough. Was it the loss of their mother which still went so deep? Were they unable to get over her death in the car accident?

'You lost your mother, didn't you, Frances?' she asked gently, and this time she saw the girl flinch.

'Yes.'

'I'm sorry.'

Frances hung up her tea towel.

'As I said before, Mrs Lacey,' she said, clearly, 'you know nothing about it.'

And Deborah felt as though a door had been slammed in her face.

★　★　★

On Thursday evening Deborah left Rory and Frances sitting watching television, while Amy was in bed.

'I'm going into Douglas to see friends of mine, John and Margaret Carlie. John was the senior partner in the firm in Athol Street where my husband worked.'

This information seemed to be of little interest to either of them, and again Deborah felt a prickle of irritation. Indifference was worse than hostility, she was beginning to feel.

'They have a daughter, June, about your age, Frances. She's taking a commercial course and is going to help out at the office.'

'I may do that some time,' said Frances, surprisingly.

Only Margaret was at home, and Deborah felt rather thankful as she relaxed in their comfortable lounge and kicked off her shoes.

'I don't know that I haven't made a mistake, Margaret,' she confided. 'I should have trained as a social worker, not a teacher, in order to handle Rory and Frances.'

'I can't understand why the girl has to stay here as well,' Margaret said, deciding that a glass of sherry might not be a bad thing. 'Surely at her age she'd be better in Glasgow getting on with her career. It isn't as though she has to take the boy about.'

'No.' Deborah frowned thoughtfully. 'But although she wasn't in the accident, I think she's been badly hurt just the same by her mother's death. It was only two years ago and she would be sixteen at the time . . . very young to lose her mother, yet old enough to appreciate the tragedy of it all. For a while Rory's life hung in the balance, too, don't forget, so maybe she wants to make it up to him in some way. He depends on her for companionship after all.'

'Plenty of young people of his own age for companionship on the island.'

'Yes, but that's what he's hiding from . . . the sympathy of his friends.'

'He . . . ' Margaret stopped. 'Oh well, we can't all be alike, and who am I to judge? I've never been in such a situation.'

'Nor I.' Deborah put down her sherry glass. 'I thought it was bad enough losing Patrick, but if I needed something to help me get over it, then the children have done that. I shan't ever forget Patrick, but I can think of him without pain now.'

'I wonder if June could help,' mused Margaret. 'Start taking Frances about, maybe, and meet a new set of friends.'

'I don't know. Rory might then want another bolthole. He wanted the north of Scotland, or one of the Western Isles, you know.'

'Then why choose here?'

'I gather that was Mr Nesbit's idea. He and his wife met here during the war.'

'Men!' said Margaret. 'Is that why the children don't settle?'

'Could be.'

Coming away Deborah forgot her cardigan, which surprised her. She was sure she had put it near her coat where she was not likely to forget it. Next day Margaret rang up to say she would send it over, and Deborah put down the telephone, frowning a little. She must be getting very absent-minded.

That afternoon Deborah managed to coax Frances into going shopping with her to Douglas. Rory didn't want to go out. He had gradually been spending more and more time in the study, lifting down Patrick's old books and leafing over the pages.

'Will you be here when Amy gets home, then?' Deborah asked. 'She's much too young to be on her own.'

'Of course,' Rory told her.

In spite of himself, the little girl was worming her way into his affections, though Deborah pretended not to notice the rather odd friendship which was growing up. It was Rory who often obliged Amy by reading the fairy tales she never tired of hearing, and Deborah wondered if the Buggane was becoming as much a part of the boy's world as her daughter's.

When she had first come to live on the Isle of Man, she had sensed the air of magic about the place, and gradually it had spun itself round her, as a spider spinning its web. In this she had delighted Patrick, who loved the old folklore. Perhaps it was no bad thing for Rory to get to know the island through that same folklore.

Frances, too, was looking a little better as they walked through the streets of Douglas, and Deborah saw her studying some serviceable jeans and shirts. The young girl was only eighteen, but there was something adult about her, as though she had never really had her adolescent years. Growing up had been thrust on her, and Deborah wondered if that had been caused by having to take her mother's place at sixteen. She rarely spoke about the aunt who had taken over the household.

But if so, Deborah vowed that she would gradually encourage her to be young again, and have some of the fun she had missed.

Yet even as they window-shopped, then called in at stores for necessary purchases, Deborah could feel the young girl's uneasiness about leaving Rory troubling her.

'Amy will be home shortly,' said Deborah. 'He won't be alone for long. She'll have him bandaging her teddy in no time.'

Frances managed a little smile. At least she wasn't jealous of the child, thought Deborah thankfully.

* * *

Yet at that moment Rory was not alone, though Frances would have been anxious if she had seen him walk the floor in the emptiness of the house which was still a little strange to him, but gradually becoming familiar.

Then the bell shrilled, and he shrank a little and waited, wondering if he need answer the door. Yet it might be the girl who brought Amy home. She might be early today.

Hesitantly Rory went to open the door, stepping back when he saw a young fair girl with healthy windblown cheeks and eyes as blue as forget-me-nots, on the doorstep.

'Hello. Are you Rory? I'm June Carlie. Can I come in?'

Who was June Carlie? wondered Rory stupidly. Yet the name seemed familiar. And she knew about him.

'Deborah left her cardigan in our house last night. I've brought it back in this carrier. Is she in?'

'No, she's out shopping, with my sister.'

'What a pity. I wanted to meet your sister.' She noticed his bewilderment, and laughed as she sat down, thoroughly at home. 'I'm sorry, I forgot. I've been coming here since Patrick Lacey became my father's partner.'

'Ah yes, of course,' said Rory, forgetting to shy away, as he normally did with strangers.

'I suppose this is your house now, and I hope you don't mind my sitting on your settee.'

'It doesn't feel like my house!'

'I wish it were mine,' said June, deliberately refusing to hear the bitter tones. So Rory Nesbit didn't like it here!

'Was your sister in the accident, too?' she asked, and Rory drew in his breath. He wasn't used to such frankness.

'No.'

'Then she's lucky not to have her face marked. It doesn't matter for a boy, but it does, rather, for a girl.'

'Doesn't . . . doesn't matter!'

'Well, maybe a bit, at first, while it hurts. But I think that in the days when men fought duels and got scars all over their faces, they got quite proud of them. They were probably romantic, so maybe that's why a scar can look romantic on a boy but not on a girl.'

'You call this romantic!' cried Rory, turning his face round to show her the livid weal of the burn which seemed to be taking months to heal.

'Oh, not at the moment,' said June cheerfully, 'In fact, it looks rather awful. But it won't always look like that, and I bet it's better than it was.'

Rory scowled. Who did this girl think she was, talking to him like this? He was more used to a brief mention, if anything was said at all.

'Anyway,' she was rattling on, 'I thought that if you wanted to join anything . . . swimming, tennis, boating, fishing . . . golf?'

'No,' said Rory, then in a softer tone, 'thank you.'

'Your sister then, if you're going to mope at home.'

'I'm not moping. I have work to do. I . . . I'm writing. At the moment I need to know about law.'

'Oh, good. I know a bit about that with going to work for Father.'

'That's rather different.'

'Maybe. But it's a common interest. Like writing, too, perhaps. I mean, writing biographies is rather different from writing children's fairy tales.' She was picking up Amy's favourite book. 'But all writers can join the same society and no doubt enjoy talking shop at meetings. Or so I should think.'

There was an interruption when the back door opened and a breathless young girl appeared with Amy.

'Here she is, Mrs Lacey,' she called. 'See you tomorrow. Cheerio, Amy.'

'Mrs Lacey isn't at home, but thank you,' shouted Rory as the door closed and Amy danced in.

'Hello, darling,' said June.

'Hello, June.'

Amy ran to hug the other girl, then turned to give Rory the same treatment.

'We went for a nature walk,' she informed him, 'and I got a flower for you, Rory.'

He took the tiny, rather battered yellow flower awkwardly, flushing at the amusement on June Carlie's face.

'At least you aren't able to beat all the girls off, Rory,' she said teasingly. 'There's always one who keeps trying.'

She jumped to her feet.

'No use waiting then, if Deborah and your sister are going to take ages. If it's a fine day on Saturday, shall I bring my swim suit, and we can go down to the cove? The weather's warming up now, though you have to be hardy. And I'm hardy.'

She looked magnificent, thought Rory painfully, standing there with her long fair hair, shining eyes and wonderful complexion. And she hadn't shrunk from him. But maybe Deborah Lacey had asked her to come. Maybe she'd taken Frances out of the way, and left her cardigan behind last night to make an excuse for the girl. She was so beastly well-meaning.

'Please yourself,' he said sullenly.

'Thank you for being so gracious about it,' said June, her smile fading and her eyes sparking a little. 'If you want to make friends on the island, then you'll have to be willing to *be* a friend.'

He was about to point out that he was getting away from friends, not bent on making new ones, but a look at her face soon had him holding his tongue.

'I shall only come if you're going to be pleased to see me. Believe me, I've plenty to do without running after you, especially if I'm not wanted.'

She turned to go, and he put out his hand.

'No . . . look, I'm sorry. It's . . . nice of you. Come on Saturday.'

He had said it with an effort, but she took it at its face value and gave him a brilliant smile.

'That's better. Tell your sister I look forward to seeing her. 'Bye, Amy darling. See you Saturday, Rory.'

She was gone, leaving a faint perfume which made Rory think of lilacs in the rain. What would Frances say? he wondered uneasily. Somehow he didn't want her to hurt June Carlie in any way.

It didn't occur to him that for the first time in months he was more worried about hurting someone else than in being hurt himself!

4

Mark Nesbit arrived at the weekend and Deborah found that a great deal of time had to be spent sorting out legal matters. She felt a qualm of fear when the last signature had been made, but Mark seemed to understand that this might be so, and turned to her reassuringly.

'You'll never know how grateful I am to have your help.'

'So long as it is help,' she said, rather ruefully. 'Sometimes I feel that I shan't ever help the children to settle. They . . . they seem to be taking a long time to . . . to get over the loss of their mother.'

Mark's face closed a little.

'Yes,' he said briefly.

'I'm sorry, I didn't want to pry.'

He turned away.

'What about your husband's books?

Do you want them to remain where they are at the moment?'

'Oh yes. I think Rory enjoys peeping into them.'

He stood for a moment, hands in pockets, at his favourite position in front of the large bay window, with the wonderful view of the sea.

'The children loved their mother,' he said at length, 'but it was only after . . . after she was killed that I realised she had such a hold on them. Rory's grief was far more for her than for himself. And Frances . . . well, she changed from an average child of her age, I suppose, all wrapped up in her own affairs, to the girl you see now, fussing over Rory and unable to think what she wants to do herself. She planned to come into my office, but that seems to have gone by the board. She dropped all her old friends, and she just seems to drift. There's been no other woman I could turn to . . . for advice. Not even my sister Marion. I thought a woman might understand her.'

'Have you seen your doctor?'

'Yes. He's overworked. He could find nothing wrong with her, except that she'd had an upset and time would put that right. He gave her a tonic and suggested a holiday.'

'Wouldn't they be better separated?'

'I tried that, but it didn't work. Frances feels she just has to help Rory.'

'I've insisted that she helps me in the house,' Deborah told him, 'and that Rory does some work. I . . . I feel I can't cope, just leaving them to their own devices. They'll have to co-operate.'

'Of course.' He turned to look at her. 'Have I been very unfair in asking you, a stranger, to do this for me?'

She was aware of his sudden appeal and had a queer feeling that if she met it, there might be some new subtle change in their relationship, as though she would be committed to him and his family for always. Deborah felt herself withdrawing, wanting to cling to her own freedom and independence.

'I'm being well paid,' she said evenly, and he drew back.

'Oh, of course. I . . . er . . . I'm glad the arrangements suit you.'

'And I'm afraid they're going to be meeting young people again. It's very difficult to shut out the world, especially here, and a very small part of it has already sought them out.' He raised his eyebrows. 'I mean June Carlie, daughter of Patrick's partner, John Carlie. She came here the other day to return a cardigan I left at their house, and talked to Rory. She's coming back today . . . to go swimming, I understand. June is very down-to-earth. I don't know how well she and Frances will hit it off, but I gather she's bulldozed Rory into allowing her to come. They're going down to the cove.'

'I'll be interested to see if Miss June Carlie comes back for another visit,' said Mark.

Deborah nodded. That would be the real test.

* * *

If June found that the welcome she
received from Frances was rather cool,
she gave no sign of it as she offered her
hand in a firm handshake. There was a
marked contrast between the two girls,
thought Deborah, with Frances being
so delicately made, her dark hair falling
softly about her small pointed face.
June was much taller, her hair very fair
against the warm apricot of her skin.
Even their vivid blue eyes held a subtle
change of tone.

'It's cold for bathing, surely,' objected
Frances when Rory explained that June
wanted to go to the cove.

'Nonsense, it's a gorgeous day,' said
June, throwing back her head and
turning to look at Rory. 'There's a
breeze, but it won't chill us down. The
sea will be warm enough. I often take
Amy at this time of year, don't I, pet?'

'Can I come now?' asked the child
eagerly.

Frances was still frowning, but it was

she who agreed to look after Amy.

'All right, you two can swim. I'll come down with Amy.'

Deborah felt a momentary qualm. She hadn't, as yet, allowed Amy to go swimming without being there herself to see to the child, even when June took her.

'I don't know, darling,' she said hesitantly. 'I . . . '

'Don't you think I can look after her?' demanded Frances bluntly, and Deborah decided that she was turning into a fussy mother.

'Of course,' she agreed quietly. 'I'll get her swim suit and a towel.'

Frances didn't quite know what to make of June Carlie as they made their way down to the cove.

'You need some sunburn on you, Rory,' she said, eyeing his pale back frankly. 'If you get browned up, that scar won't show half as much.'

Frances looked to see if Rory was wincing away, but he seemed to be taking the remark in his stride.

'He could do with playing tennis, too, or some other sort of game,' June continued, turning to Frances. 'It would strengthen up his body again, after being in a hospital bed for so long.'

'Rory had internal injuries . . . ' Frances said coldly.

'You didn't tell me that.' June's voice was accusing.

'I'm better now.'

'Well, there you are, then. You've just got to find out what's harmful to you and what isn't. How long are you staying, Frances? Are you having time off from college or your job?'

'I've no job at the moment,' said Frances stiffly, 'I'm helping to look after Rory.'

'He looks as though he'll be looking after himself soon. You ought to get a job on the island. It's gorgeous in summer, even when storms blow up. You just want to see the sea lashing against the rocks as though it would batter the whole island to pieces. It's glorious.'

'It sounds heavenly,' said Frances, with a touch of sarcasm which June refused to notice.

'And if you haven't been far, I shall take you all over the island, and introduce you to the fairies, though you'll have to treat them properly, Frances, or they may think you're one of their rivals!'

'You don't believe that stuff!' laughed Rory, and again Frances darted a look at him. He was laughing! He *couldn't* have forgotten . . .

June was laughing, too.

'Race you in!' she was saying, and a moment later they had dived into the sea.

'Us now,' said Amy. 'Us, too, Frances.'

'What? In a moment,' she said absently, sitting down to pluck at a blade of grass, but instead of seeing the gentle surge of the waves and the cries of the gulls overhead, she was sitting beside a hospital bed, with Rory there, his face and head bound in bandages.

Her mother, she knew, was dead.

'She found out, Frances,' Rory was mumbling. 'I had to tell her. She was livid. She drove like . . . like a maniac. I . . . I tried to stop her . . . '

Frances bent forward, her head in her arms to blot out the sunshine. She welcomed the dark. Only the dark was quiet enough to hide in. The sunshine brought out people, people everywhere, who could look at her and see her for what she was, then look at Rory and pity him for what she did to him.

Only Amy could sit beside her without developing that knowing, adult curiosity which could sear her soul. Only Amy . . .

Frances' head jerked. Where was Amy? Her eyes blinked blindly until they focussed properly in the glare of the sunshine. There was no sign of Rory and June, and she knew they must have swum out of sight, then she saw the small figure of the child as she stood on a rock well out into the bay.

'Stay there, Amy!' she yelled. 'Stay

71

there! Frances is coming!'

The child turned to wave happily, but her small feet seemed to slide on the rock, and Frances stifled a scream as she watched the tiny girl hit the water.

It was a nightmare. She screamed for Rory and June, but it was she herself who first reached the child, though the minutes that it took to get there were hours long, as she remembered that each one was precious and might mean the difference between life and death.

Then Rory and June were there, helping her to bring the limp child ashore, and Rory was competently taking charge. They had both learned life-saving, and it was June who had to stand aside and watch, her eyes full of fear, while they worked steadily to revive the child.

June ran ahead of them while Rory carried Amy, then Mark was there, and Deborah whose eyes, for one long moment, looked at Frances.

'She's all right,' said Rory weakly. 'Best get the doctor to make sure.'

June saw Frances running, almost stumbling ahead of them to the house, and caught up with her.

'It could happen to anyone,' she said, panting. 'Don't go blaming yourself too much, though it's good to blame yourself a little, and watch out for it so that there isn't ever a next time.'

'Leave me alone!' cried Frances, and June looked at her tormented eyes. 'Leave me alone. I . . . I'm not fit to be in charge of her . . . of anyone.'

'You're certainly not fit to be in charge of Rory,' said June, rather brutally, 'but I think you'd be the finest person ever to be in charge of Amy from now on.'

'Stop blabbing on,' cried Frances. 'You don't know what I am.'

'I know you love wallowing in your own self-loathing. It's written all over you. You enjoy it. All right, go on. Have yourself a lovely time and enjoy your own self-hatred.'

'Get away from me!' said Frances furiously. 'I don't want to see anyone.'

She stayed upstairs for the rest of the day until at length Deborah could bring herself to go and talk to her, though it was through a locked door.

'Amy's fine, Frances,' she said clearly. 'The doctor has been. I know you let her get too far ahead of you, but you did get her out of the sea. And you and Rory saved her life. I . . . I'll always remember that.'

The door didn't open, but when Amy had had her bath in the evening and was being taken along to her bedroom, she banged on the door.

'Read me a story, Frances,' she called. 'Read me about Robin the Fiddler. Frances! Frances!'

The door opened and closed again swiftly behind the child, and Deborah, standing outside, went quietly back to the bathroom and gathered up Amy's soiled clothing.

Next morning she came downstairs as usual, without referring to the incident, and it seemed to Deborah that she was no different from usual, accepting her household duties without question.

But if anything, the outer shell was just a little harder.

The weather began to grow warm with the cool breeze softening, so that the days were clear, bright and languid. Frances was spending all her free time at the cove, often alone if Rory was busy, and in spite of herself, she began to love the quiet peaceful beauty of the place, and to feel that it was hers. Theirs was the nearest house, and few visitors ever came that way, so that when she arrived there one morning and found the bronzed figure of a young man sitting on her favourite patch of grass, she felt unreasonably annoyed.

'Oh!'

She pulled up short from her scramble down the cliff path, and he rolled over lazily and stared back at her, then nodded.

'Hello. Lovely day.'

'Yes.'

75

Frances wished the cove was part of their property, then she could order this interloper to remove himself, but, chagrined, she knew that she would have to put up with him. He was probably a summer visitor to Laxey village, and that meant it might be all of a fortnight before she had the place to herself again. The advent of summer brought tourists to the island and selfishly she decided there would be no peace till they all went away again.

He was looking at her as though he had seen the place first, too, and resented her intrusion, so her chin firmed and she found another patch of grass and spread out her bathing wrap to sit on, then produced her book. If he thought *she* was moving, then he could think again!

Yet it was hard not to think of him sitting nearby, his own book open beside him, while he carefully filled a pipe with tobacco. He looked as though he had already had a holiday, she thought, seeing his bronzed shoulders.

Most people were as pale-skinned as she and Rory had been when they first came.

She tried to concentrate on her book, wishing he would take the hint and go, but finally he broke the silence with a loud sigh.

'Are you here on holiday, Miss . . . ?'

Her chin lifted and she smiled rather condescendingly.

'No, I live here.'

She was immediately aware, with satisfaction, of his quickening interest.

'Oh?'

'Yes.'

He put the pipe in his mouth, lit it and puffed thoughtfully.

'Are *you* here on holiday?' she countered.

'No. I live here, too.'

Frances felt her smile waver and she sat up and looked at the strange young man. By now she had surely met all the young people in her neighbourhood.

'I thought I knew everyone here,' she said flatly.

'So did I. Which particular house is now your home?'

'The nearest one.'

'Rock House? Where Mrs Lacey lives?'

'Yes. My father bought it, and my brother and I live there. Mrs Lacey has stayed on as our housekeeper.'

'I haven't been home long enough to pick up that piece of gossip,' the young man grinned, 'though no doubt I shall hear all about you over lunch. We're neighbours. I'm Paul Denham from Hillcrest, just further up the hill.'

'Paul Denham? I . . . I didn't know Mr and Mrs Denham had a son. I . . . I thought they'd just retired to Hillcrest.'

'It was my grandparents' home, then when they died, Mother let it for a few years. A couple of years ago, Father retired early through ill-health and when the house came up for re-letting, they decided to come here. I've been away at college.'

'Oh, I see,' she said, rather grudgingly, not liking the information at all.

The cove was no longer hers. Obviously this young man . . . Paul Denham . . . had also staked a claim on it. And if he lived here, then she would have him using it all the time. Was there nowhere she could be on her own?

Something of her feelings must have shown on her face, because Paul Denham was grinning at her maddeningly.

'Sorry if I've pinched your retreat, but it's been mine, too, ever since I can remember. I used to stay with Grandma and Grandfather during the school holidays. I can't blame anyone for loving it, and wanting it for their own.'

'I don't love it,' she said quickly, then amended that, knowing it wasn't really the truth. 'Well, maybe I do a bit . . . '

'Why did you come, then?'

'Because I had no choice,' she said defiantly, 'and anyway, it's . . . ' She stopped and picked up her book.

'None of my business,' he finished. 'I'm afraid my biggest fault is incurable curiosity about other people. I'm sorry.'

'I must get back,' Frances said, standing up.

She had intended to sit it out and not let any stranger drive her from *her* cove. But this man wasn't a stranger. He had been coming here all his life. *She* felt as though she was the interloper.

'You've only just come. Don't run away,' he said, his eyes laughing.

'No, I have to go. I . . . er . . . I've things to do. In the house.'

'You have to help Mrs Lacey?'

She lifted her chin again.

'I'm mistress of the house. I . . . er . . . I have to organise things. Mrs Lacey is the housekeeper.'

'Of course,' he agreed solemnly.

'I have to look after my brother, and Father comes as often as he can at weekends.'

'Then he doesn't work on the island?'

'No. In Glasgow. Our proper home is in Glasgow.'

Again his eyes gleamed.

'I see. Ah well, so it's goodbye for the time being. Or au revoir. Perhaps I shall see you here tomorrow morning?'

She hesitated. It would be like cutting her nose off if she didn't come at all, just because he was here. She had already talked much more to him than she had intended, but of course, she need only acknowledge his presence, then go in swimming, or read a little.

'Perhaps,' she agreed.

He stood up and she saw that he towered over her, a very large young man with a pleasant bronzed face, light brown curly hair and large brown eyes which could be full of laughter or deep penetration.

'You didn't tell me your name.'

'Frances Nesbit.'

'Frances . . . a nice name. Till tomorrow, then. Cheerio.'

'Cheerio,' she echoed, rather foolishly, and found her way back up the cliff path, feeling ruffled and out of sorts, yet strangely alive. The dead feeling which had been with her since Amy's accident was beginning to lift.

Though Paul Denham was a disturbance, just as June Carlie had been. Gradually their peace and quiet was going to be whittled away, though it was inevitable here, she thought. Northern Scotland would have been best, or an island rather less accessible. There was going to be little isolation here!

★ ★ ★

Frances was rather quiet and thoughtful for the rest of the day, and helped Deborah to wash up after tea, a job which she didn't insist that Frances shared.

'I didn't know Mr and Mrs Denham had a son,' she said diffidently.

'Oh, is Paul home? Have you met him, then?'

'Yes, today. Down at the cove.'

'The Denhams didn't have Paul till they'd been married some years. I rather think they're the kind of people that find their only child so precious that they *can't* talk about him, if you know what I mean. They hug their pride to themselves. Did he tell you about himself?'

'A bit. Not much. He . . . he wants me to go there again tomorrow.'

'Are you going?' asked Deborah casually.

'I don't know.'

'I should think that of all the friends you could have, Paul Denham is the best.'

'I don't want to get involved with new friends. I just want to have time to myself, and so does Rory. I hope June Carlie won't keep making a nuisance of herself.'

'June would be the last person to do that.'

Deborah put away some plates.

'What are you afraid of, Frances?' she asked quietly. 'What worries you so much?'

'Nothing worries me,' Frances said quickly, 'only Rory getting better, that's all.'

'Surely he'd get better much more

quickly if you encouraged him to be sociable. I can understand your friends in Glasgow offering sympathy which he felt he didn't want, but no one here knows what Rory, or you, were like before the accident, so you won't get the same degree of sympathy, especially if you don't court it.'

'They ask questions,' said Frances sulkily. 'I hate being asked questions about Rory . . . and about Mother . . . '

Her voice trembled a little, and on impulse Deborah put an arm round her shoulders.

'Can't you learn to accept what happened?' she asked gently. 'Your mother wouldn't want to see you living with so much grief . . . '

'Oh, leave me alone!' cried Frances. 'That's what I mean by well-meaning strangers all asking questions, all deciding that they can help with a few words of comfort. They think they know it all, just by listening to a few details. But they know so little it's . . . it's laughable!'

Deborah drew back, feeling clumsy and stupid, and shut out from the real facts. And how could she be expected to help Frances and Rory regain their happiness and well-being, if she didn't know those real facts?

'And you won't tell me about it?' she asked.

Her nature and instinct was to keep out of it all and allow Frances to get over it in her own way, but her sense of responsibility to this family who now employed her was beginning to grow strong. It *was* her affair, she argued with herself, whether she liked it or not.

'Why?' asked Frances. 'What could you do, except . . . except . . . ' She broke off, and a moment later Amy came into the kitchen.

'I've lost Teddy,' she complained, her eyes rather heavy and sleepy.

'He's in the doll's pram.'

'He's not! He's not in my dolly's pram.'

'I'll help you find him,' said Frances

quickly, obviously glad of the interruption.

Deborah watched them go, then went to where Rory was tidying away some papers. He seemed to be doing a great deal of home study, though he had merely smiled a little when she tried to show that she was willing to be interested. He probably looked on her as archaic, thought Deborah wryly.

'I'm going for a walk,' he told her, 'while it's still fine.'

'You may meet Paul Denham, home from College,' Deborah told him, smiling. 'Mr and Mrs Denham from Hillcrest . . . their son. Frances and he met today.'

'She didn't say anything about it,' said Rory, almost accusingly.

'She will. She's having to find Teddy for Amy.'

He said no more, and swung on his anorak round his shoulders. Deborah felt tired, and she was grateful when Frances offered to bath Amy and put her to bed.

It was two weeks now since Mark Nesbit had been home, and she found herself hoping that he would come on Friday evening.

Just so that they could talk over a few problems, she assured herself hastily. Nothing more than that.

5

Next morning Frances struggled with herself, and lost. Towards mid-morning she put on her prettiest sunbathing dress and picked up her book, saying she would be back soon. Deborah watched her go, a smile in her eyes, though she carefully made no comment.

There was no one already taking up space on Frances' favourite grassy slope, and unreasonably she was as disappointed today as she had been the previous day, but for the opposite reason. She had been looking forward to seeing Paul Denham again, but obviously their encounter had not meant quite so much to him.

Proudly she made her way to her usual spot and sat down, spreading out her towel, suntan lotion, sunglasses and her book. She should be glad things were back to normal.

Her dark hair fell forward on to her cheeks, the ends curling and bright with the gloss of extra brushing, though that had been for the good of her hair, she assured herself, not for any other reason.

Half an hour later she felt bored with her own company, though that hadn't happened to her for a long time, and she collected her belongings irritably and rose to her feet, just as the tall bronzed figure of Paul Denham appeared on the cliff path.

'Hello there,' he called. 'Not going, surely!'

'I've been out long enough,' she said briefly.

'And I've only just managed to get away,' he grinned. 'I helped Dad with a job which couldn't be left half finished, but as soon as I could, I told him I had a date with a charming lady, and he agreed that I must keep it.'

'There was no need to hurry on my account,' she said stiffly.

'Ah, but I had to hurry on my own. A date is a date. You could have changed your mind and I'd have been disappointed, but if I'd broken my promise, then I'd have been even more disappointed. Do I make sense?'

'Sort of.'

She looked at him curiously. He was different from any of the other young men she knew, but she couldn't put her finger on the difference. He was as tall as Rory, but not so dark, with curly hair and laughing brown eyes. He had good teeth and a rather short snub nose which Frances found rather disarming.

'Then sit down again for a moment. Tell me about yourself.'

Immediately her face closed.

'There's nothing to tell. My . . . my brother was in a car accident, and is recovering. He . . . his face has been scarred . . . '

'Oh, poor chap! Too bad. I must call on him and see . . . '

'He came here to be on his own.'

He was silent and she felt the words

hanging between them.

'I'm sorry. That sounded rude.'

'You speak your mind and I like that. I shall always know where I stand with you. I shan't call on your brother if you don't wish it, but I'd like you to ask him if I may call. Perhaps he *would* like a visitor. You never know. Will you ask him?'

'Oh, all right. And he's had a visitor, if you must know. A girl from Douglas called June Carlie.'

Instantly the brown eyes lit up in a smile.

'June! Good for her. Your brother couldn't have a more delightful visitor.'

'You know her?'

'Certainly I do. She's one of my special people.'

Frances felt an odd twinge which she recognised as jealousy. She looked around for her book and spectacles. There was no point in sitting here talking to Paul Denham. It was just going to make a complication in her life, and it was best to keep away now before she would be swept along like that plastic cup being swept in on the tide.

'Oh dear, I can't keep you at all,' said Paul ruefully. 'Still, we have a whole month in which to get acquainted.'

'A month?'

'My last fling before the cares and responsibilities of my job settle on my shoulders, which are likely to become bowed under the weight.'

In spite of herself Frances smiled. She couldn't imagine him taking on too much responsibility with his first job.

'What sort of job?' she asked. 'Is it here on the island?'

'No to the second question. It's in Manchester. And as to what sort of job, didn't Mrs Lacey tell you all about it?'

'I didn't ask her,' she said stiffly, then blushed. She *had* asked Deborah in an oblique way, about Paul.

'Then I'll tell you all about it, but not today. It will be for our more serious moments, and today we are just enjoying the sunshine, and the blue of the sea, and the gulls crying overhead, and listening to the heart-beats of the island. Can't you hear it pulsing away? Oh, but I forgot, you're too new to hear it calling to you. After a while it may speak to you, but only if you love it. Have you explored it all yet?'

'No.'

'What? Haven't you spread your wings at all, like a fairy, and gone out to enjoy the richness of it all? Instead you've been like a little brownie, hiding behind toadstools and afraid of seeing and being seen.'

'I didn't feel like going very far and Rory . . . Rory is having to take things easy. He's studying law, so he can do that, quietly at home. I think he's going to try writing a thriller, though Father hopes he'll try for university when his health permits.'

'Good for him. What about you?'

'I'll probably go back to Glasgow and help Daddy in the office, as June Carlie is doing in her father's office.'

She mentioned the other girl's name again, almost deliberately, and saw his eyes soften again as he grinned.

'Competent girl, June. You could do worse than follow her pattern. Can't I call for you tomorrow?'

'No,' she said quickly. 'Daddy will be home. He might want to go out or something.'

The smile faded a little.

'All right, Frances, I'll stay away.'

'Can't we go on Monday?' she asked impulsively. 'Could we go to Peel . . . somewhere on the other side of the island? I know Laxey village and Douglas now, so there's no need to take me to see that huge waterwheel!'

He grinned. 'All right. We'll go in my old car, if you like, though we must treat her gently. She's at a time of life when frailty has set in, and I need her in Manchester.'

'That will be fine.'

'Come in and say hello to my folks. They think you're a shy young fawn whom they've rarely met.'

But she had taken enough steps out of line.

'Not today, please. Another time. Though your mother . . . and your father . . . I like them. They're very charming.'

She was a trifle breathless, and he laughed again.

'Then your visit to Hillcrest is only postponed.'

'Yes,' she agreed.

Back home she found June installed in the sitting-room, arguing with Rory, and a sight of the lovely fair girl whom Paul obviously admired roused jealousy in Frances again. No doubt she and Paul had plenty in common. They were both island people, and would understand one another. And they had both taken it upon themselves to befriend the newcomers. That showed that they were alike in nature as well.

Now June was berating Rory as Paul had berated her.

'Your face will get better just as quickly playing tennis as stuck here.

What does the doctor say? Surely a little healthy exercise won't be bad.'

'Leave Rory alone,' broke in Frances. 'He doesn't feel like strenuous games.'

'Maybe tennis is a bit strenuous,' June conceded mildly. 'Swimming, then, Rory. Or even walking. Come on, get some fresh air into your lungs . . . '

'Rory doesn't want people staring . . . ' Frances cut in, and this time June's eyes grew cool. She looked evenly at Frances and deliberately turned again to Rory who was sprawling on the settee, surveying the toes of his shoes moodily.

'I came to ask you to come out with me, Rory,' June said quietly. 'If you don't want to, then say so, but don't let Frances keep saying it for you.'

Both Rory and Frances coloured rosily, and Frances had anger in her eyes.

'Of all the impertinence!'

'Is it impertinence to call on a friend? I consider that Rory is my friend, even if you don't want to be . . . or don't want him to be, either. I'd back down if I thought you were doing the best you could for him, but I think you're just keeping him back, so I'm sticking my neck out . . . '

'Oh, stop squabbling, both of you,' cried Rory, rising suddenly. 'I'm going out by myself.'

The two girls were left on their own, and June again stared levelly at Frances.

'That's not good for him either, so I'll go after him in a minute, though if it were anyone else, I'd be out of here like a shot, and minding my own business. But I happen to like Deb Lacey very much, and I've a feeling she's worried about Rory. And you should wake up, Frances, and see that you're only keeping him back, doing this hen with one chick act of yours. You should be glad to have me take an interest in what happens to him.'

'What have your other boy-friends to say about it?' asked Frances.

'Such as who?'

'Paul Denham.'

She got out the name with difficulty and saw the sunshine break out on June's face.

'Paul! Is he home? The rascal didn't tell me.' Then she turned again to Frances. 'Well, if you've been talking to Paul, it's a wonder he hasn't talked some sense into you. He's the tops.'

'Mutual admiration society!'

'I've no doubt. And he's still the tops, so don't forget it. For now I'm going after Rory. He'll have to forget all about that scar, then maybe it will go away . . .'

'How can you say that!'

'Or fade into insignificance . . . same thing in the end. Only I'm out to heal the inside part first. Why can't you wish me luck?'

'Because it's Rory I care about.'

'Same thing,' said June again, grinning. 'Did he ever tell you to run away and play with your own friends when you were children?'

'Frequently. But then things were different.'

'Perhaps not so different as all that. We've been rotten to each other, but we might grow to like one another. Cheerio, Frances.'

She went out and Frances saw the breeze blowing tendrils of fair hair across her forehead as she passed the window, and she felt her anger boiling. June Carlie set her teeth on edge.

Deborah came home a short while later with Amy, and she soon noticed that Frances was put out about something, though she spoke pleasantly about other matters.

'Amy wants a birthday party next month. Think we could cope with eight children, Frances? I'm afraid I've always been whacked before, when I was brave enough to invite a few of the little ones for tea.'

Frances managed to smile. Deborah had noticed many times that she was good with children when she forgot to be wrapped up in herself. No doubt that was why she had taken it so hard when Amy fell into the sea.

'If she's good, we might think about it,' she agreed, and was treated to a bear's hug by the little girl.

'I love Frances,' Amy announced, and the girl coloured furiously and drew away.

'June Carlie's been here. She's chasing Rory,' she told Deborah.

'Nice for Rory!'

'Is it? She might make him dependent on her, then get bored with her own good intentions and he . . . he . . . ' She stopped. 'He'll be back like he was in Glasgow,' she finished, in a low voice.

'Surely all young people aren't so irresponsible. I shouldn't have thought June was, and Paul certainly isn't. Didn't you have any steadfast friends in Glasgow?'

'Only those who were always drooling over Rory. Two girls he'd been friendly with before the accident. They gushed all over him. Roger Curtis, his best friend, has already done a year at university, and he was away when it happened. He looked sick when he saw

Rory and Rory minded. He'd rather not see Roger now.'

'It isn't good for him to shut off his friends,' said Deborah gently. 'Or you. Haven't you any old friends you'd like to invite over, perhaps for a few days during the summer months? Amy can come in with me, and even though her bedroom is tiny, I'm sure a young boy or girl wouldn't mind, for the sake of a holiday here, on the island.'

But Frances had gone white.

'I've no friends I'd care to ask,' she said, very quietly. 'Thank you just the same.'

Deborah's eyes were troubled as she made tea, putting out one more cup for June. If she knew June, she wouldn't be so easily put off, and it seemed to her that June only saw what she wanted to see in Rory. Scars would soon heal, and could be disregarded.

Yet it was odd that Frances had dropped her friends, too. She could understand Rory, especially if he was aware of constant pity.

But Frances was a puzzle. Surely she would want to keep her friends, even if she didn't bring them to the house. It was one more thing she wanted to talk over with Mark, and again she hoped he would come that weekend. There was something quite comforting about Mark Nesbit's presence in the house.

6

The routine of Mark Nesbit's life had altered considerably, and at first he found it a bewildering experience, returning each evening from the office of his engineering works in the city, to a house which was now empty for the first time since his marriage. His housekeeper no longer lived in, having now gone to live with her daughter ever since a baby was born, though she arrived each morning in time to cook his breakfast.

Mark ran the administrative end of the engineering company, while Robert McLean's word was law on the shop floor. It was only a small works, but it had taken all their energy and drive over the years to become established. In recent years the hard work had paid off, and at least Una had not needed to economise since the children were very much younger. Mark had often been thankful that she had enjoyed several prosperous years before her death.

Yet those years were not the ones he liked to remember with nostalgia. Comfortable means had tended to make Una discontented, and often he had fought down irritation when she decided to make changes in the home, because one of her friends had already bought something new which she considered to be so much better than her own. Their comfortable old plush suite was exchanged for a new one in dralon because it would be so much easier to keep clean. Mark admired the new rose pink suite, but the old wine-coloured one had worn itself into the right shape round his body.

Una had tired of clothes as quickly, or even more quickly than she tired of furniture, and her wardrobe still bulged with expensive suits and furs. Mark had removed the jewellery to the bank. Some day he hoped Frances would be able to go through her mother's personal things. There might be some items she would want to keep, but while she still grieved, he couldn't even suggest such a thing. No doubt as Rory's health improved, so would Frances put it all behind her, and live her own life again.

Towards the end of each week, Mark usually found himself looking forward to the trip over to the Isle of Man even if it was a tiring journey, and one he couldn't undertake every weekend. Sometimes it fitted in well with business commitments, and sometimes not at all.

He missed the children very much, which was no doubt why he was beginning to think of Rock House as more like his home than his own house in Glasgow. Though, of course, there was no doubt that Deborah Lacey was a fine housekeeper, and his weekends were spent in comfort, and an easing of the heart of which he was only vaguely aware.

He liked the old chintz-covered

armchairs and settees at the island house so much better than the immaculate new ones of his own home. There he could don his old sweater, pick up a favourite book and relax for an hour.

Nor did he find himself constantly on edge because of tensions growing up among the children. Of course one could not expect all problems to be solved immediately, but he was sure that Rory looked better. Frances, too.

On Saturday afternoon they had both gone out, and Mrs Lacey peeped into the sitting-room to see Mark relaxing with his book. Amy had gone to play with a few of her friends, so Deborah quickly set a tea tray for both of them, and carried it into the lounge.

'May I join you, Mr Nesbit?' she asked quietly.

He smiled, his eyes crinkling.

'I should be offended if you didn't want to do so. It will give me an opportunity to say all over again how grateful I am that you decided to help me out as you have done. It seems to be working so well. Rory is quite brown and the scar marks so much less noticeable.'

'The worst ones don't show at all,' Deborah said, very quietly. 'That's what I want to talk to you about.'

'You mean, he's being difficult?' asked Mark, his face sobering.

'Not Rory. Frances.'

Mark was silent as he accepted a cup of tea with sugar and lemon.

'Frances? But . . . but she's just here to help Rory. I thought I made it clear she wasn't involved in the accident. Her main upset was losing her mother, but time is passing. She should be putting it all behind her as she grows older.'

'Should, but isn't,' said Deborah gently. 'There must have been a very strong bond between her and her mother, Mr Nesbit . . . '

'Please, call me Mark if you will. I can only talk to you if you're willing to be a friend.'

A faint touch of colour tinted her cheeks.

'My name is Deborah, though Patrick called me Deb or Debbie.'

'I like the whole name,' Mark told her. 'It suits you.'

She smiled, but returned to the matter which was troubling her.

'We've talked about this before, Mr . . . Mark, but I didn't realise how unhappy Frances is underneath. Have you always had the same doctor in Glasgow?'

'Yes. He's known Frances since she was a baby.'

'Then couldn't you take her along to see him again? I know you said he's overworked, but I think her nerves have been upset over this. I think she needs more than a tonic!'

He hesitated for a while.

'Don't you think it would be even more upsetting if I suddenly took her away from the island again? I mean, I could see she was strung up and nervy, but I thought this . . . this enforced idleness would relax her down.'

He was unaware of the sudden

fatigue in his voice, as though he had carried the load on him for too long, and Deborah felt she wanted to put out a soothing hand, and tell him to forget it all for now. Yet if Frances was brooding about something, deep down, then harm could be done by evading the issue.

Frances had been quiet and thoughtful over the past day or two, saying little when she returned from sunbathing, and even avoiding Rory. Deborah would like to have known if she was seeing Paul Denham, but she never forced Frances' confidence. She preferred that the girl should come to her.

'Let's forget about it over the weekend,' she said at length, feeling that Mark, too, needed some sort of respite. For a moment her heart was sad, as she thought of how Patrick had slipped away from her life, hers and Amy's, and how after her initial grief and the weeks of aching loneliness and loss, she had come to terms with herself, and could now think of him sadly, but without pain.

Yet how much more disruption there had been in the Nesbit family, when Una Nesbit was killed. Perhaps it was because Una had been lost by accident, whereas with Patrick it had been the outcome of illness.

'If the children are seeing to their own affairs, perhaps you and I could take Amy on a picnic tomorrow to some other part of the island,' Mark suggested.

Deborah felt her heart warming. It would be nice to go out again on an outing like that.

'It would be lovely,' she agreed.

'Hello there, you two!'

Deborah looked round swiftly as Frances appeared from the direction of the back door, and her eyes widened at the sight. She could see the small frown of worry ease from Mark's forehead as he sat up and looked at his daughter. Because this was the old Frances he could scarcely remember, and a lovely happy girl Deborah had not yet seen.

'Paul's here,' she told them. 'He

wants to meet Daddy.'

'I can only stay for a moment,' Paul Denham told them, bringing up the rear. 'I have to get back home.'

'Long enough for a cup of tea, Paul, surely.'

'All right, Mrs Lacey,' he grinned, and held out a strong hand for Mark's warm handshake.

Deborah walked to the kitchen, thinking how strange it was that a topsy-turvy world could right itself so quickly. Love was a great worker of miracles, and even if she didn't yet acknowledge it herself, she could see that Frances had fallen in love with Paul Denham. And Paul had never been one to seek out any special girl. Deborah prayed that Frances be the one to hold his heart. Surely of all the young men she could have met, Paul was the most suitable to keep her the happy girl she looked today.

But later Deborah was to remember that moment, and to wonder at how wrong she had been. And to wonder at how quickly one's world could turn upside down again!

Frances found herself looking forward more and more to her meetings with Paul Denham. At first she had felt the lightheartedness and casual air of the friendship he offered, but gradually she felt that he was beginning to see her as a real person. Theirs was not a friendship to be made quickly, and as quickly forgotten.

Together they began to roam over the island. Paul had a bicycle and, with a smile, Mrs Denham found an old upright one with cord laced through the back mudguards.

'That was to prevent our skirts being caught in the wheels,' Mrs Denham explained, her eyes dancing. 'Hardly a problem for the young lady of today.'

Frances looked down at her own brief shorts and grinned, then laughed even more when she looked again at the old bike. It would be even more fun than Paul's old car.

'No, it isn't, is it?'

'Good thing too! You'll be more comfortable in those, Frances, so long as you can keep the midges at bay. Paul, you'd best check this over, though I've always kept it in good condition.'

'Mother always looks after things even when they've ceased to be of much use to her. The piano gets tuned regularly . . . '

'I *do* play a little, darling.'

' . . . and no doubt her tennis racket is in excellent condition and her long striped swimsuit all washed and pressed . . . '

'That's enough, Paul. I thought your new sense of responsibility might have changed you, but it hasn't.'

They were grinning at one another and Frances felt a sudden pang of longing, though she hardly knew for what. There seemed to be such a warm happy relationship between Paul and his mother, yet she could only stand outside it, looking in.

She felt herself being drawn into the warmth of his companionship, and

113

something in her told her to resist it, so that at times she grew cool and brusque with him. Apart from an eyebrow quirked in her direction, however, he would take it all in his stride, as though accepting everything about her as part of her, and therefore acceptable to him.

Paul had checked over the bicycle, and she had had a few hilarious moments trying to ride the old machine while he fell about laughing. But at last she felt able to ride it properly, and together they explored an island which was full of enchantment, as she learned to look at it through Paul's eyes. Already she knew a great many of the fairy tales of mermaids and fairy people which she had to read to Amy over and over again, and Paul didn't laugh and tease her when she confided that she almost felt that the people she had read about were real.

'I was brought up on them, too,' he told her gently.

She loved going to watch the fishing boats, and walking with bare feet through the rich green grass or sitting on a rock dangling her feet in the warmth of the sea while the breeze lifted her curtain of hair gently about her cheeks.

On the day after Paul had met Mark, he was rather quiet as they found their way to their favourite spot by the cove near Rock House.

He lay flat out chewing a piece of grass, his eyes on the faint outline of the Cumberland hills. The past few weeks had passed so quickly, ever since he had first met Frances, then Rory.

'I shall be going soon,' he told her, and her heart suddenly went cold as she sat up and looked at him. She had buried her head in the sand, she thought, biting her lip. She had been content to let the days slide past like sand slipping through her fingers, but she had sifted nothing from the sand. Soon there would be nothing left.

'I hope we won't ever lose touch with one another.'

Frances was very still. Was she

entitled to put out a hand, to make the step forward to meet Paul a little? He was different from anyone she had ever met before, and there was an elusive difference she couldn't quite fathom. It was some quality she had felt in him right from the beginning.

He had told her a great deal about his childhood, his hopes and fears of adolescence, and the many pleasures they could share together, at the moment. But he rarely spoke of his future and she had not probed.

But now she was curious about the job he was going to do in Manchester, a job he had promised to tell her all about some day before he went back.

'You could write to me,' she suggested.

'Only if you want my letters. Perhaps I shall be very glad of your letters when I'm walking along the wet streets of Manchester, though I'm sure it doesn't always rain, as people say. There will be days of sunshine as well, days when I'll be thinking of you.' She looked back at him gravely. 'You won't mind if I think about you?'

She shook her head. 'I don't know.'

'Did someone hurt you, Frances?'

Her face paled. 'I hurt myself.'

'Couldn't you tell me about it? Couldn't I help to make it better? After all, it's my . . . ' he stopped.

'Your what?'

'My life, I suppose . . . my job. If I can't help us, who can I help?'

Frances groaned.

'You never discuss your job, Paul. You said you'd tell me what you were going to do, though if it's some sort of Government secret, then of course I won't expect you to . . . '

'No, it's nothing like that. I wanted you to get to know me better for myself. Sometimes . . . sometimes a dog collar puts one on the other side of the fence, as it were . . . '

'A dog collar?' She sat up, and as she understood, the blood drained from her face, leaving her eyes flashing blue lights. 'You're a priest!'

'A curate. I should have told you, I

know, but this past week or two . . . it's been like something precious snatched from time. I thought it was that way for us both, Frances . . . '

'But now your job is coming out on top,' she said harshly. 'Now you feel . . . feel the sin in me, and want to start work putting it right!'

'What sin?' He looked bewildered.

'Oh, don't pretend, Paul. You've just asked me to tell you what's wrong, haven't you? Well, I can handle it for myself, thank you very much. No one can help me. I have to live with myself, that's what.'

'I don't understand.'

Paul put out a hand, but she ignored it and got to her feet.

'Goodbye, Paul. It's been nice, hasn't it? I . . . I hope you'll be . . . successful in Manchester. Good luck!'

She picked up her bag and ran lightly towards the cliff path, and he stood watching her, unable to fathom what had happened, except that she must have rejected him because of his calling.

He sat a long time having an inner battle with himself, then stood up, his eyes a little bleak. When he arrived home, only his mother could see that something had happened.

'I'll have to gather my books together,' he said quietly. 'There's only a few more days now.'

'I've checked over your clothes, dear,' she told him. 'I'll help you to pack.'

'Thanks, Mother.'

Frances had hurt him, she thought bleakly. It just didn't seem possible that he could have hurt Frances.

★　★　★

Deborah was quick to sense the change in Frances, and she felt keenly disappointed. For a short while it had seemed as though Mark's experiment in bringing his children to the island in order to help them find themselves again had succeeded. But now it looked as though Frances was more unhappy than ever. It was easy to guess that the reason for this was Paul Denham, but Deborah knew that the underlying cause went much deeper.

'You didn't tell me he was a priest,' Frances said, almost accusingly, as she helped with the washing up.

'It was up to Paul to tell you about himself,' Deborah told her, and Frances said nothing more for a moment.

'I wonder why he didn't,' Deborah said musingly.

'He said that his collar sometimes put him behind a fence to other people. He wanted me to get to know him first.'

'Then it seems to me it shouldn't make any difference.'

'I don't want to talk about it.' Frances put away the last of the cups, and walked out of the kitchen, but as she turned to go, Deborah caught sight of tears in her eyes, which shook her a little. She had never seen Frances in tears, however upset she had been.

When Mark came the following weekend, she was rather despondent.

'I'm afraid I'm not being of much

help to you after all, Mark,' Deborah told him, when they went for a stroll that evening after Amy had gone to bed. 'I think you need a friend who has known Frances all her life, or almost all her life, someone who knew her before the accident, and who might find the right words to say to her. Sometimes I think I only make things worse.'

'That's nonsense,' said Mark, 'and I don't know any friend who could help, unless . . . ' He paused for a moment. 'She did know someone quite well . . . a neighbour's son who used to coach her at tennis, though he was a great deal older than she. In his thirties, maybe. Lionel Wright. I think he was like a Dutch uncle to her, if you know what I mean.'

'Someone she respected?'

'Oh, very much. He used to take an interest in both children, but Rory got sick of hearing his name, I think. He was a technical representative in a Glasgow firm dealing in some sort of synthetics, but he was transferred to

London shortly before the accident . . . or it may have been after. After, I think, because I remember him visiting Rory in hospital. At any rate, I haven't seen him for a long time, and Frances didn't seem to bother about Lionel, probably because she gave up playing tennis. Besides, I doubt if he would remember a young girl in Glasgow after he settled down in London.'

'He wasn't married, then?'

Mark shook his head.

'Not at that time, but there was talk that a girl had once let him down. I remember Frances being indignant on his behalf.'

Deborah nodded. It was interesting to hear about the girl's past interests and friends, but she really wanted to hear more about Una Nesbit, and somehow she couldn't make the first step forward in asking Mark about his dead wife.

'Was she . . . well, very happy up until the time of the accident? Happy at home?' Deborah suddenly felt that the question might seem a little impertinent. 'I mean, Frances was only sixteen then, and sometimes girls go through a difficult phase at that age. Sometimes the smallest of problems get blown up into big ones.'

Mark frowned.

'Oh yes, she was happy,' he told her. 'I wasn't at home a great deal, and Una led a busy life, too. She was always being asked on to committees and to help organise charitable events.'

'And Frances helped her?'

'Only with school affairs.'

'I see.'

Again Deborah was silent, trying to picture Mark's life as it had been two years ago. She felt she wanted to know a great deal more about Una Nesbit, but when Mark talked about her, it was usually about the early days of their marriage, and especially about the time they had spent on the Isle of Man during the war. Often she could feel the spirit of the young Una walking beside them as they walked down to Onchan, or wandered about on the beach at Douglas.

'I wonder if she would have liked those horse-drawn trams,' Mark had mused. 'There was nothing like that when we were here before.'

It was easy to see that the early years of Mark's marriage had been happy, but what of the later years? Had they been drifting apart a little? wondered Deborah. Had the pressures of earning the family income, building up their home and bringing up their family come between their own close relationship? It was hard to keep a close relationship in marriage, if one was an individual, she thought, remembering the days when she herself felt lonely but Patrick was well absorbed in his books and papers. She'd had Amy, and it was easy to take Amy out on her own without trying to get Patrick to come with them.

Perhaps they, too, would have drifted apart if their marriage had lasted a long time, thought Deborah with a sigh.

She glanced at Mark Nesbit, seeing that he looked very much stronger and fitter than Patrick. She was getting used to his thin brown face with his thatch of dark hair growing a little grey, and suddenly she sensed that she was no longer lonely when this man was around. She was beginning to depend on him, she realised with a rush of dismay, and that wasn't a good thing at all. Before he came she had felt that she was finding her feet as a single person again. In marriage one tended to let go of one's independence, then when one was left alone, the loneliness could be quite frightening.

It had taken her a few weeks to learn to be herself again, and to depend only on herself for her emotional as well as her practical life. But now, without knowing it, she had been looking forward more and more to Mark's visits every other week, thinking it was because for that brief time, she could share the responsibility of Rory and Frances.

But it had been for herself, too, she thought with a pang. She had been learning to look forward to seeing him again for her own sake.

'What's wrong? What are you thinking?' asked Mark, hearing her small intake of breath.

'You . . . your wife must have been a very popular person,' she said, snatching at the conversation they'd been having.

'Oh, yes, she was that all right,' Mark agreed.

'You must miss her . . . even more than the children miss her.'

'A home can be very bleak without a woman in it,' Mark said. 'It's very quiet, in Glasgow. But I look forward very much to coming here. There's always that.'

'Yes, you still have Frances,' she agreed.

'And you!'

The words seemed to hang between them.

'That's not quite the same,' said

Deborah quietly, not looking at him.

'No, nothing's the same. Not even that. Sometimes one makes a mess of things, too. We should remember that, and not wish for . . . ' He broke off abruptly.

'Wish for what? she asked.

'The moon,' he grinned. 'Don't you think one can get awfully moonstruck here? Shall I ask Rory? He seems very friendly with young June.'

The mood was broken and Deborah laughed with him. It seemed odd that she had been wary of how to handle Rory when he first came, because under the companionship of June, he was growing more and more into an ordinary young man of his generation.

She was unaware that Frances had seen Paul Denham saying his goodbyes to some friends who had obviously called at Hillcrest the previous evening. Frances had been out walking by herself and had been drawn, as though by a magnet, to look up at their neighbour's house in the moonlight, hearing the faint sounds of laughter from within, knowing that it was Paul's last evening. He was coming to take a formal leave of them all in the morning, but she wouldn't be seeing him alone.

But as she walked in the evening, she hadn't known what she wanted, only that she was conscious of an overwhelming longing for him to sense her presence outside, and slip away so that they could be together. Somehow, magically, they could erase the past few days and she could go back to thinking of Paul as just Paul, and not the Reverend Paul Denham.

But it couldn't be erased, she thought, standing on a headland and listening to the soft surge of the sea below. She could no more stop the onward marching of time than she could the ebb and flow of the sea. Paul Denham had chosen to be a priest, and some day, if he should choose a woman to be his partner . . . his wife . . . then he would choose a woman who was as good and lovely inside as out. It would be a woman who would have had more foresight than to get mixed up in an affair, as she had done, without thought to the possible consequences.

Because her mother had got to hear of it and had driven off in a rage to do something about it, with Rory by her side, she . . . she . . .

Frances had leaned against a wooden post, shutting her eyes as she always did, to shut out her own thoughts. It was then that the door of Hillcrest had opened, and several people had come out, talking and laughing, while the Denhams waved them away in their cars.

Last of all there had been June Carlie, and Paul had talked to her for longer, his parents having gone inside. Frances had wanted to move on, but she was afraid the movement would draw attention to herself, so she stayed where she was, silent, but unable to tear her eyes away. She loved Paul Denham with fierce longing, and also with tenderness which told her that it would last for always.

But now he was saying goodbye to another girl, a girl worthy of him, whom he had known all his life.

June got into her car and wound down the window, and Frances watched as Paul bent and kissed her quickly, then waved her away. He stood for a long moment, silhouetted against the light from the house, then slowly went indoors, and Frances hung on to her wooden post for a moment longer as reaction set in, and waves of jealousy swept over her.

June Carlie! Pretending to be so interested in Rory, too! Making him dependent on her, then dropping him no doubt! She had thought June good enough for Paul with her straight, fearless gaze and fresh young body. But she was every bit as . . . as rotten as Frances herself.

Though there was no blood on June's hands, thought Frances blackly, trudging home. Especially not that of her own mother.

7

'Letter for you, Rory.'

Deborah knocked lightly on the study door, and walked in with the letter to where Rory sat, working at his desk. For a while he had doggedly persisted with his writing, short stories and articles, sending them out to various papers and magazines whose addresses he had found in the 'Writers and Artists Year Book', and with unfailing regularity they had all come back again. Deborah had carried the bulky envelopes back into the study, unsure whether to offer him the sympathy and support she felt, or to keep out of it.

Finally, one morning, seeing the defeat in his eyes and the ugly scar on his cheek standing out more prominently than usual, she had sat down on the chair opposite the desk, as she had done many times with Patrick.

'I'm losing it all,' he told her. 'I . . . I thought that when I started to sell one or two articles and a story, I would keep on doing so, and that it would build up, but instead I've lost it . . . lost the little I had.'

'I know very little about journalism, Rory . . .'

'It isn't really journalism, but I know nothing about it either, or so it would seem.'

'Something, surely, when you have already made some sales. Can't you go back and look . . . try to see what was in them to make them attractive to editors, while these later ones are not? Could it be that, perhaps, they meet the market requirements very much better? I mean, could they have been more suitable for the requirements of the paper?'

'Or could it be that I'm completely out of touch?' asked Rory bitterly, 'living in a cocoon?'

'You'd have been more in a cocoon living in the far north, surely, seeing no one. That was what you wanted, wasn't it?'

He said nothing, but stared moodily at his returned manuscripts.

'Well, it seems that I can't write here.'

Deborah got up, feeling that she knew too little about it to help Rory. She sighed, feeling completely unfitted to help either of the young people in any way, and had sudden sympathy for him again. They were both facing a brick wall.

'I'll fetch you a cup of coffee, dear,' she said quietly, 'and have one myself. Maybe it will make us both feel better.'

He looked up and it was as though she had struck the right note between them, and he was conscious of her genuine interest in him, with regard which had been slowly building up.

'Thanks, Deb.'

When she returned with the coffee, he was poring over some papers and magazines, several discarded manuscripts scattered on the desk.

133

'You know, you had a point, Deborah,' he told her. 'I've been trying too hard to be original and say things completely new. Only they were so original that they fitted in with nothing, if you know what I mean. I . . . I suppose one must be original . . . but within a certain framework.'

Eagerly he began showing her his papers, manuscripts and other magazines.

'This one fitted in. I remember thinking that it probably would, when I wrote it. And it was a good idea.' His enthusiasm wavered a little. 'I don't seem to have had any good ideas for ages.'

'But you will again,' she encouraged him. 'Can't you look at your stories again? See what went wrong?'

'Maybe.'

'Couldn't a good agent help? Someone who would know what was needed better than you?'

Again she could see his enthusiasm kindling.

'I could try.'

She said nothing, afraid of shattering the fragile thing which was his hope, and in many ways also her hope.

'I'll leave you to it, then, Rory.'

After that he had allowed her to share in what he was doing, though she noticed that he put it carefully behind him when June called, or when Frances wanted to talk to him.

But now, at last, a small letter had come for Rory, and she carried it in, as casually as she could, but her heart beating as wildly in hope as she knew his must be. Their eyes met, in understanding, even as he opened it, then he was round the desk and whirling her madly round the room.

'What on earth — ?' asked Frances, at the door.

'An acceptance,' Rory told her. 'For another short story. Twenty pounds!'

Frances looked at both Rory and Deborah, their faces shining with pleasure.

'Congratulations,' she said huskily.

'Deb's been helping me. I was about ready to throw in the sponge. I must telephone June . . . tell her the good news.'

Frances' face had changed and she stood looking at Deborah after Rory had walked out into the hall and picked up the telephone. Deborah saw the misery in the girl's eyes, and her heart sank afresh. She was making headway now, with Rory, but it looked as though Frances was further away than ever. Surely the girl couldn't be jealous of her, because Rory had been willing to accept her help, however little it had been.

'Frances . . . ' she said, taking a step forward, even as they heard his eager voice on the telephone, 'I didn't do much for Rory, I'm afraid. The credit is all his.'

The young girl looked at her.

'Everything is a mess,' she said. 'A mess. I'm going to tell Daddy he's got to get us out of here and back home again.'

Rory had heard the last part of her conversation as he came back into the study.

'What's got into you?' he asked, in disbelief. 'What mess? And why should we want to get away from here? May I remind you that it was as much for your benefit as mine that we wanted to get away! As far as I'm concerned, it's beginning to sort itself out, for the first time in months. So include me out.'

'You're a fool!' she flared at him. 'You can't see a thing, even when it's under your nose.'

'What can't I see? I can see that you've just been trying to make big troubles out of little ones. What has happened is past. We've got to put it behind us.'

'You can, but you know it's different for me. Only I won't stand by and see you hoodwinked.'

'Who by, for heaven's sake? And if you want to move from here, then move. But I'm beginning to find my feet. I like this island. It's beautiful, and it's got peace and quiet without complete isolation.'

'And its women know how to get their man!'

Deborah didn't wait to hear more. The brother and sister often had small quarrels, but they had been little more than childish squabbles. But this one was different. This one showed that Frances was slipping further and further away from her, even as she had felt some success with Rory.

And what did she mean, that the women of the island knew how to get their man? It couldn't be . . .

Deborah stopped short, her heart lurching suddenly. Mark Nesbit had been making regular weekend visits, and almost unconsciously she had been making special efforts to make the house more comfortable for him. There had been extra cleaning and polishing, the kitchen filled with a smell of baking, and a small posy of flowers put in his bedroom.

She had assured herself that this was

a housekeeper's job, keeping her employer's home comfortable and attractive, and that the extra effort was just to prove to him that this was so. And when he did come, she had just been happy to fall in with whatever wish he had to make, either sitting comfortably by the fireside while they talked, or walking miles along the headland.

Last visit the T.T. Races had been on, and they had taken Frances and Amy to watch, the excitement of the crowds infectious, so that Deborah's hair had blown in the wind and she looked young and carefree as a girl. Rory had preferred to go with June and a few of her friends, and Frances had opted out of the young people's party. Now Deborah wondered, her cheeks flaming scarlet, if this was because she had wanted to keep an eye on her and her father! Did Frances feel that their friendship was beginning to be too close?

Well, she needn't, thought Deborah indignantly. If Frances thought she was an 'island woman out to get her man', then she had another think coming! And how dared she even suggest such a thing about the girls who had befriended her on the island, girls like June and her young friends!

Righteous anger outweighed any compassion Deborah had been beginning to feel for Frances, and she felt that if the girl *did* want to speak to Mark about moving away, then she would encourage her. She would be jolly glad to be rid of her.

But that would mean Rory going, too . . . just when she had started to make a little headway. It was beginning to mean more to her than she realised, to turn Rory into a whole young man again, with so little regard for the scar which had marred him inside as well as out, that it would soon heal, also inside as well as out. Already she felt that it was healing inside.

But even as Deborah's thoughts whirled round again, as she beat up the pancake mixture which had always been a fine palliative for hurt rage, Deborah's deeply rooted honesty began to surface, and with sick shock she realised that there might be something in Frances' fears.

She *had* been looking forward to seeing Mark. She had acknowledged, quite openly, that the house felt different while he was here. She had been remembering his tall, dynamic figure with the slightly stooped shoulders, his hair greying a little above his forehead, his brows wrinkled in thought. She was seeing him much more clearly, now, than she could see Patrick, and he was making an even bigger mark on her life than Patrick had ever done.

Had Frances sensed something that she hadn't even dared acknowledge to herself, that she was falling in love with Mark Nesbit?

Deborah beat up the pancake batter faster than ever, her cheeks scarlet. Had Mark guessed, too? Somehow she must stop all this now, before she got any more involved.

Yet if she did, what would she and Amy do now? There was Amy to be considered, too. Deborah could feel the unfamiliar tears welling again. She had only managed to cry for Patrick, and even when things were black, before Mark came, she had faced it all, dry-eyed.

She would do nothing in a hurry. She needed time to think. Yet time could also be her enemy, taking with it her last shreds of independence so that she and Amy might face hardship very soon. There wasn't much money for real independence.

Frances was right. It *was* a mess!

★ ★ ★

'What was all that about?' asked Rory.

'Never mind.'

Reaction was setting in, and Frances was ashamed. She should be glad for Rory that he was beginning to find happiness again. And if he started selling his writing, and perhaps even books, he might be famous one day, when he probably wouldn't care if June Carlie *did* let him down. In fact, she would probably want to keep hanging round him, now that he was beginning to look so much better.

Frances remembered her sight of him as he danced round with Deborah, and his scar hadn't looked too bad. His skin was becoming darkly tanned, and soon it would just be giving him an interesting look.

'I'm glad about your story,' she said sincerely. 'Are you going to do more now?'

'You bet! Nose to the grindstone from now on, *and* I'm trying a book. Not that it will be much good as yet, but I'll get the feel of it and learn how long it takes to write a full novel, and how much physical effort there is in it, as well as mental. Deb says she'll help me with the typing.'

'So will I,' offered Frances eagerly. 'I mean, there must be times when she's busy, and I'm not.'

'That's what's wrong with you,' said Rory. 'You're not half busy enough. Why don't you get a job? Like June. She could help you there.'

But mention of June had brought the closed look back to Frances' face, and Rory caught her arm.

'Come on, out with it. What's up? Why the displeasure over June?'

'Let go of me, Rory.'

'Not until you tell me. If you weren't you, I'd think you were jealous, though heaven knows why you should be jealous of June.'

She said nothing, but the colour glowed in her face, and Rory stared.

'You *are* jealous,' he accused, 'and . . . and it can't be because of me. You never care a hoot how many girls I've taken out. And what was all that about the girls on the island knowing how to get their man? I thought Deborah looked fed up with you over that.'

'Deborah!'

'Yes. I mean, she lives here all the time. Always. This is her island, as it were, and you're criticising her people. She was probably very hurt.'

Again Frances coloured. She didn't want to hurt Deborah, on whom she had almost unconsciously come to depend. Yet how could she apologise without complaining about June? And the Carlies were friends of Deborah's.

'Oh, lor',' she said. 'I never thought. I was only . . . grousing.'

'What about? It was something to do with June.'

'I saw her . . . with Paul . . . ' she said defiantly. 'I . . . I think there's something between them.'

'They've been friends all their lives,' said Rory calmly, 'and if you think I'm breaking my heart if June ever went off with someone else, you've got it all wrong, Frances. I know people say there can't be just ordinary friendship between a man and a girl, but a girl like June *can* be a pal. She's been a great help to me, but we haven't fallen for each other, if that's what's worrying you.' He stared at her searchingly. 'Of

145

course! I see it now. It's Paul Denham.'

'Shut up, Rory.'

'You've fallen for him.'

'I haven't!'

Her voice choked, and Rory was suddenly gentle.

'What's the matter, Fran? I thought you'd got him bowled over, too. He was showing all the signs when he said goodbye to us all, and you wouldn't even take the hint to see him off on your own. I felt like kicking you.'

'He's a priest, Rory.'

Frances stared at him, the tears welling, and he sat down suddenly.

'A priest! You mean, like a monk or something . . . never getting married? Celibate, isn't it?'

'No, he's a curate in the Church of England. He . . . he can get married, if he wants. In fact, I think it's better if they do, then the vicar's wife can help in the parish. That sort of thing.'

'And . . . and he doesn't care enough for you?'

Her head went down.

'I . . . I think he does, or did anyway. He . . . he said . . . ' She stopped and bit her lip. 'Never mind what he said. That was between me and him, and I can't even tell you.'

'Then I don't see the problem, or why you're jealous of June, unless you feel she'd make a better lady of the parish than you. Is that why you're jealous of her?'

'Don't be so thick!' she flared. 'Sometimes I think the accident shook up your common sense. How . . . how could I go to Paul after . . . after what happened . . . ? And him a priest!'

Rory was silent, his eyes brooding.

'I've said it before, and the more I think about it, the more I think I'm right. You make too much of it, Frances. Even if Mother hadn't found out, and you were stopped because . . . because of the accident, I don't think you'd have gone through with it anyway. You were only a child — sixteen. *He's* the one to blame, almost old enough to be your father, from what you told me.'

147

'But I was running away with him, wasn't I? I'd got my case with me. We were going to London, Rory. I . . . I can hardly believe now that I could be that stupid, but I really thought I was in love, and that there was no one like him. I know that if we'd stayed at home, Mother and Dad would just have parted us. His parents, too. They'd all have thought it ridiculous.'

'Which it was. I told you that at the time.'

'I know.' Frances' eyes looked haunted. 'It's awful how it looks from now, and it's just a nightmare when I think about Mother . . . '

'Well, it's my fault, too. I needn't have told her where you were, but I did. I knew she'd stop you, even if I couldn't. Only she drove like a maniac, and when she screeched round a corner and . . . and I thought she was going to knock someone over, I . . . I grabbed at the wheel. It was my fault, too, Frances.'

'You paid. Just look at your face.

148

I . . . I feel as though I'm responsible for that, too. And I've got nothing, nothing to bear as a punishment. Unless it's losing Paul.'

'But he'd understand. I mean, you *were* stopped. It isn't as though you did go off with him. You only got as far as the station. Thank goodness old Lionel saw you there, just after he'd seen the accident.'

'Yes,' Frances agreed, her face sickly pale with memory. 'Daddy never found out what I was doing there, and I couldn't tell him. They were always so busy, he and Mummy. He didn't know half of what went on at home. He just thought I was off to stay with a girl friend.'

'That's what I mean. Nobody knows, and even I never knew who the man was. It was the one thing you wouldn't tell me, and that frightened me more than anything. Can't you tell me even now?'

She shook her head, her face paper white.

149

'I don't want anyone to know. If I tell no one, then I might manage to forget about him some day, and not feel so ashamed.'

'Then why can't you marry Paul if he asks you?'

'You don't know a thing about your own sister. How could I marry Paul, even if he did want me, without telling him? I mean, a parson's wife has to be like Caesar's wife, hasn't she? And if I told him, it would always hang between us. If . . . if it hadn't been for the accident, it might have been all right . . . just a silly girl's mistake . . . but the consequences of that mistake are there, and always will be. That's no small thing to be forgotten quickly.'

Rory understood.

'I . . . I guess I've no right to be jealous of June, or anyone else, but I couldn't help it. Men often have a special love for girls they've known all their lives, even if it's different from other sorts of love. I . . . I suppose that I felt if I could hate June for a while, I'd

150

maybe stop hating myself.'

'Do you still think about the other man? You don't love him now, do you? I wish I'd got to know him at least.'

Her eyes darkened.

'I try not to think about him, but when I do, I'm almost sick. Looking back on it I can see that he . . . he was rotten. He was older than I, and . . . and spun me such tales, like a spider spinning its web round a fly. I was fairly caught, Rory. I mean, some girls are old at sixteen, but Mummy kept me like a child. I was hardly allowed to decide anything for myself, so I had no sense of proportion, and no judgement.'

'Maybe she realised that, when she found out,' said Rory soberly. 'She kept blaming herself. I . . . I think that's why she drove so fast, as though some dreadful fear or anger was overcoming her.'

'I can't forget her, or forgive myself,' said Frances, 'and most of all I wish I could forget *him*. At least I don't have to see him here. That's why I won't tell even you!'

'No. I did plenty of agitating to get away, for you as well as me, in case you *did* get pestered. Though, come to think of it, that might have been a mistake.'

'I felt that he was always hovering just out of range, and I'd never get rid of him. I couldn't explain to Daddy. Thank heavens he never knew. Promise you'll never tell him, Rory.'

'Do you think I'm a halfwit?'

'Just look at the time! I haven't helped Deborah with lunch. I'll have to rush, Rory.'

Deborah was annoyed, thought Frances, chastened, when she appeared in the kitchen.

'I've attended to everything,' she told Frances crisply. 'After all, it's my job.'

'Oh,' said Frances, rather lamely.

'I'll wash up.'

'You needn't . . . '

'No, I insist. I must do something. Oh, is it pancakes for afters? Rory will be pleased.'

'Yes, it's pancakes,' said Deborah flatly.

* * *

Mark often liked to walk through the streets of Douglas and along the promenade alone, before going on to Rock House. It was becoming the only way he could remember his marriage, with all the love he had cherished for Una. He liked to look up at the hotels in which their units had been billeted during the war, and sometimes at the other hotels which had been full of internees, the barbed wire an insurmountable barrier which seemed to symbolise their lives and his own.

But now even those far-off days, which he had remembered with such clarity, were becoming dulled and distant, like the pursuit of dreams. He and Una had been separated while their love was as tender and delicate as a young plant, he to go abroad, and she transferred back to the mainland.

They had written regularly, long letters to be cherished, read and re-read. She had always been there, waiting for him, while he travelled over North Africa, Italy, then on to the Middle East.

They had been married when he came home on an extended leave in 1945, but the years following his release from the Army, the years to which they had both looked forward so eagerly, had been disappointing. Mark sighed, remembering the lean times, the anxieties and frustrations. Una had refused to have a family until they had settled down and his business was beginning to prosper. She wanted a home of her own, as beautiful as his parents' home which later came to them. It had to be beautiful enough to entertain her friends, and the efforts to achieve this had tired them both. In fact, it was only later, after his parents died and they came to the old family home, that Una felt they had something worthy of them and a good enough background for him. And slowly his business had prospered, and they had become solid citizens.

But something had been lost from those early courtship days, which he now looked on as carefree though they didn't seem so at the time. The wonder, the excitement had gone . . . the romance, perhaps . . . the indefinable something which gave the days an aura of enchantment which he later came to connect with the island. He had wanted to come back many times, but Una refused to come. Perhaps she had been right. Perhaps, if they could not recapture the golden thread which had snapped somewhere, then they might have been forced to acknowledge something best left unsaid.

They had been married for seven years when Rory was born, then Frances only two years later, and for a while Mark had been very happy, though the strain of keeping the family budget well supplied had been great. Una could not manage two small children by herself, and run their home so that it was still well cared for and attractive to the friends she loved to entertain.

She had become a person in her own right, and not just Mrs Mark Nesbit. The years brought maturity and the sort of graceful competence which comes with experience, and Una had been sought after more and more, to help with charities and many other social activities.

She had taken it all in her stride, assuring him that her efforts would be helpful to him, if indirectly, and helpful to the children who still had to find their feet.

Yet something had been missing, and Mark often tortured himself, wondering where the elusive, precious bond which had once been between them, had gone. When had it been lost? When he had said goodbye to Una on this very island?

Mark walked along the promenade, his coat collar turned up against the wind and rain. He had remembered such days, when the sea lashed against the walls, throwing small pebbles on to the pavement, with pleasure and excitement, because they were all part of the ideal he had found on the island. He wondered if he had expected too much, even believing that it would be possible to keep it for always.

Weren't most families exactly like theirs had been? He loved his children, as had Una, but somewhere between childhood and adolescence, he had lost his understanding of them. They had all become separate people, living under the same roof, so that now he couldn't reach them. Their thoughts, fears, worries, pleasures were unknown to him.

He stood looking out at the angry sea, the rain refreshing on his hair and face, knowing that he would be wet through before he reached home.

Home. He savoured the word. Gradually the house at the top of the bay was becoming more like home to him than the one which had always been his home, and his heart pained him. This shouldn't be so.

He had tried to tell himself that it was because his children were there, and perhaps because of the hold the island had on his heart. But his own honesty was forcing him to admit that the real reason lay in the quiet young woman, with the straight level look in her eyes, who had slipped into his life. He was falling in love with Deborah Lacey.

That wasn't quite right either. He was already deeply in love with Deborah Lacey. He loved everything about her, her quiet ways, her competence, her beauty, and her daughter as his own daughter. The child was becoming very dear to his heart.

But although she was a widow, she was also a young woman, much younger than he. He wouldn't expect her to be similarly attracted. He was fast approaching middle age, and he had two grown-up children.

Mark shivered a little, the weather no

longer refreshing, but chilling him to the bone, so that he began to make for home without losing more time. He would take a taxi, if he could find one, instead of the Ramsay bus.

Deborah scolded him for his wet state, then stopped uncomfortably when she saw that he didn't seem to mind the scolding! There was a light in his eyes, in fact, which even suggested that he might be enjoying it, and somehow that disturbed her more than anything had done.

'Rory has gone to see June,' she explained. 'I hope he has more sense than you, walking around in the rain. He's sold another story, and he wants to share the pleasure of it with June. Oh dear, perhaps he wanted to tell you himself.'

'Why?' He looked surprised.

'Because . . . ' This time it was her turn to be surprised. 'Boys like telling their parents about their successes, of course. Even small ones. Surely that's so.'

'Oh. Yes, I suppose you're right.'

But it hadn't been like that for years. He'd had to find out that Rory had written most of the school play one year by looking at the programme. Yet he had never been afraid to show his pride in the boy.

'And Frances?' he asked.

Deborah's face closed a little, and in his awareness of his love for her, he could see that all was not well between her and Frances.

'She's taken Amy to see a Walt Disney film. It . . . it was good of her to offer. Of course Amy was excited, and I . . . well, I had to let them go.'

'Didn't you want Frances to be in charge of Amy? Was that because she was careless that other time?'

'Oh no! No. In fact, because of that accident, Frances is probably the best person to be in charge of Amy. She's so determined never to let such a thing happen again.'

'Then what is it? Why shouldn't they go off to see a film, especially a Walt Disney?'

Deborah managed to smile.

'No reason at all, of course. It just seems a pity that ... that Frances hasn't a friend of her own age.'

He was looking at her shrewdly.

'She's hurt you. What has she been doing? Or was it something she said?'

Deborah flushed scarlet.

'How ... how silly,' she said, her cheeks still flushed guiltily.

'Very well. I'll get it out of her when she gets home.'

'Oh no! Please don't say anything. Only I ... I think she feels that I ... I set too much store by our ... our friendship, which is ridiculous really.'

His face had gone grave.

'I mean, it's only her young fears. No doubt she still remembers her mother with so much love that ... that she's afraid of your showing friendship to any other woman. The fact that she's been suspecting me shows how ridiculous it is.'

Mark's eyes went bleak. All unconsciously Deborah had let him know exactly how he stood with regard to her. His common sense had told him it would be like this, but his hopes had been there, too. Now they were all gone.

'She does need some friends of her own to worry about,' he said, rather harshly, angry at what he considered to be his daughter's interference. 'I'll maybe do something about that, and if it won't be too much for you, I could ask them to call some time. Some of Frances' friends have asked for her at home, and I've always rather kept her whereabouts to myself. Now I see that might not have been a good thing.'

'Of course they'll be welcome here, though . . . '

'They'd probably want to stay in Douglas,' said Mark quickly.

'Oh, of course.'

* * *

Mark had changed, and was once again comfortable in front of the fire. But

Frances' fears and remarks hung between him and Deborah, so that there wasn't the usual communication between them, and once again he felt loneliness and isolation.

Deborah, watching, could also see the barriers go up, and her own heart was heavy. So Mark was attaching importance to what Frances had said. He was also recognising that they had been becoming much too friendly, more friendly than their association warranted.

She looked at his tall figure, spread out on an easy chair before the fire, his hair still standing in small peaks because of the rain, and she forced down the sudden longing for them to be the only two people in each other's lives, even for a little while.

It seemed a very long time since she had felt the comfort of a man's arms round her, and this longing for Mark was biting deep into her heart. She wanted to smooth down his spiky hair, and feel the warmth of his long thin fingers on her own.

Instead she excused herself, saying that she had dinner to cook, and left him to doze by the fireside.

By himself, Mark's thoughts were his own.

8

Deborah's visits to the Carlies had been fewer since the Nesbits came, but on Tuesday evening she left Frances looking after Amy, and went off to see Margaret, knowing that they would have the evening to themselves. June was playing tennis, and John was attending a meeting.

'It's good to see you again, Deb,' said Margaret, with quiet satisfaction. 'You should come more often.'

'Things have changed. You forget, I'm an employed person now.'

'Oh, but surely . . . '

'Whatever the circumstances, Mark Nesbit pays me a housekeeper's salary. I can't go making use of my employer's daughter to baby-sit for me, whenever I feel the need.'

'No, I suppose not.'

Margaret's eyes grew speculative as

she went to collect a tray she had set for both of them. Deborah wasn't the relaxed and basically happy person she had been, even though she'd had worries. Now it would seem that she had swapped one set of worries for another, even if they were of a different nature.

'Rory seems a nice boy,' she said, sitting down again on the settee. 'His scar isn't really disfiguring, and when he obviously forgets about it, and talks with animation, it hardly shows at all. It's only when he broods a little and puts his fingers to his cheek that you notice.'

'June's been good for him.'

Margaret smiled. 'She hectors him, anyway. It surprises me that he takes her straightforward remarks. I don't know how I came to have a daughter who's taking such a long time to acquire tact.'

'Rory can be grateful. I think he was getting rather fed up with tact. He's sold a small article this morning, so he's happy. Now he's talking about trying to find a job on a newspaper, but he'll have to talk that over with Mark, who wants him to go to university.'

Margaret was silent, wondering if that was Deborah's problem.

'Will . . . will things change for you then, Debbie? I mean, does Mr Nesbit intend to keep on the house when Rory is well again?'

'I don't know . . . we haven't discussed it. But in any case, Margaret, I don't think it's working out.'

Margaret put down her cup. She hadn't been wrong. Deborah was unhappy in this new set-up.

'Yet you seem to have made a success of it,' she encouraged.

'With Rory, yes. But Frances . . . not with Frances.'

Margaret's eyes widened.

'But I thought she was settled, too. I mean, she came last night to see June, and to ask her about getting a job here. She thought she would like something to do. June is looking around for her.'

Deborah was surprised.

'That's what I mean, Margaret. I didn't know. Frances doesn't confide in me, not like Rory. It's ridiculous, really, but I think she . . . she suspects that I'm trying to be too friendly with . . . with Mark.'

Deborah's cheeks had coloured, and Margaret could see that she was upset.

'I would have thought her more sensible. But young girls do get funny ideas.'

She would have liked to know how Deborah *did* feel about Mark Nesbit.

'It makes things difficult.'

Deborah resorted to a very old habit, a bad habit, and tucked her thumb nail between her teeth.

'I've tried to let her see that she's all wrong, but I . . . we . . . can't discuss it openly, if you know what I mean.'

They were silent, and Margaret refilled her coffee cup.

'I shall have to get another job after all, if I find things getting too difficult,' said Deborah. 'I feel insecure, without a proper home of my own. It was a mistake, Margaret, though I didn't know what else to do at the time. But somehow I should have seen to it that Amy and I had our own home, however tiny. It can be a bit frightening, not having one's own home.'

That was something Margaret had never experienced, but she could imagine that it would be frightening.

'Look, Debbie, if you need a bolthole, then come here. Promise?'

'Oh, but I couldn't . . . '

'Even for a week or two, till you see what you want to do.'

Deborah nodded.

'All right. Thanks, Margaret. It's good to know I'd have somewhere. Has June found anything for Frances?'

'Don't think so. Not yet. But she will . . . you know June.'

Deborah's smile had more sunshine behind it.

'Yes, I know June.'

She felt better on the way home. She was prepared to sacrifice quite a bit of pride for Amy, but there always comes a point where one must make a stand, and now she could make it without hurting Amy. If Frances still continued to regard her with suspicion, then she would ask Mark to find someone else to take her place. She would make a new start, she and Amy, where there was less chance of being hurt.

* * *

'I've got a job!'

Frances looked brighter than she had done for a few weeks, though Deborah had noticed that there were two letters for her that morning, one of them with a Manchester postmark. It was easy to guess that Paul Denham had been writing to Frances, and Deborah had been pleased, hoping for some new bright thread to be woven into Frances' life, one which would bring happiness.

'Doing what?' Rory asked.

'In an office. Dogsbody, I suppose, though officially I'm a filing clerk. June

170

recommended me. At least, she found they needed a girl and told me how to apply, after finding out all about it.'

'Good old June,' said Rory.

'I'm very pleased for you, Frances,' said Deborah, and some of the reserve which she had felt towards Frances melted. This was a good sign. She felt as though their lives were beginning to turn a corner and even out into a better pattern.

The bitter unhappiness she had felt in the Nesbit children was being replaced by something new, something better.

It was a firm of insurance brokers in the same building as John Carlie's office, and Deborah knew it well.

'I can start tomorrow. What should I wear, Debbie? Will it have to be a plain skirt, or something, or doesn't it matter nowadays?'

'Judging by the clothes June used to wear to the office, I don't think it matters,' laughed Deborah. 'Amy will be missing you.'

'I'll take her out for the day,' Frances decided, 'since I'm going to be a working woman.'

How she wished Frances was always like this, thought Deborah.

In fact, Paul's letter had cheered her up as much as her job. Just for a little while, it was easy to pretend there were no problems between them. Was Rory right? she wondered. Was she making too much of a mistake which she had made when she was too young to know better?

In this mood she was seeing the way clear ahead to talk it all over with Paul. She could tell Paul all about it, and . . . and if he still wanted to be friends . . . surely he would still want to be friends? But if he didn't? If he looked at her with contempt . . .

Frances thrust the awful doubting thoughts which always struggled to the surface behind her, and went to help Amy to put on her anorak and collect a few sandwiches, and a bottle of lemonade.

'Where shall we go?' she asked.

'Port Erin. Where Robin the Fiddler lived.'

'Oh, you and your old fairy tales!' laughed Frances. She almost knew them off by heart.

It was a happy day. The island was very busy now with holidaymakers, but Frances didn't seem to care about seeing so many people crowding the streets in Douglas. The T.T. Races had finished, as had the bicycle racing, but many people had come for the sheer love of the island, and it looked almost as busy as it had been on Tinwald day.

Frances felt an inner satisfaction that she wasn't just a visitor, here to enjoy the beauty of the island. She belonged here now, and the strange elusive magic which had captured her father so many years ago was now taking hold for her. She was beginning to love the place, and she knew Rory loved it, too. She had seen it in his face one day when they raced down to the cove, and had surprised some strangers.

Rory had been put out, and for the moment Frances wondered if he was still feeling sensitive over his face, even if the scars were becoming less noticeable.

'They're only picnicking on these rocks,' she said, and a few moments later the visitors had packed up and gone.

'They've left rubbish behind,' said Rory angrily. 'Visitors! What do they care?'

'Of course they care,' said Frances.

'But they don't give themselves time to love it, so they don't care if they spoil it.'

'Oh, be fair!' Frances had protested with annoyance. 'They aren't all like that. And I can remember a time when you ... we, rather ... didn't care either.'

Rory looked shamefaced.

'I know. But that was ages ago. It's different now.'

She saw his gaze sweep round the bay, and his fingers fondle the grass underneath his hands. It was different for Rory now, and it was different for her.

There were still many small pinpricks troubling her, thought Frances. There was an emptiness, yet an urgency within her when she thought of Paul Denham. There was excitement, and apprehension, yet an inner joy and happiness such as she hadn't known for years, as though part of her had been imprisoned, and was now released.

It was a happy day which Amy, too, enjoyed to the full. They had been to the bird sanctuary on the Calf of Man, and now the child was tired but happy.

Frances had promised to bring Amy home around tea-time, as Deborah didn't like the child to be late out of bed. Amy used her childish energy to the full, but she grew peevish when she was tired.

She was very tired now as they reached home, and both she and Frances were silent as they walked up to the house, hand in hand.

175

'I hope you'll stay here for always and always,' said Amy sleepily.

'I hope so, too,' said Frances, pausing to look at the house which was now theirs. At one time she had felt an interloper in Deborah's home, but Debbie had been skilful in making them feel that it was their home now. It couldn't have been easy for her, thought Frances.

There was a car outside the door, and Frances felt her heart sink. She didn't really want to talk to any visitors.

Then Deborah was at the door, to welcome both of them home, and to take the picnic basket.

'There's a surprise waiting for you in the lounge, Frances. A friend of yours . . . a gentleman . . . has called to see you. Rory is entertaining him at the moment.'

Frances felt her heart racing. It could only be Paul. He must have bought a new car.

She was conscious only of her knees shaking as she went on into the lounge, though the colour had rushed to her cheeks and her eyes sparkled with excitement. Rory looked round, grinning.

'Paul?' she asked.

But it wasn't Paul who rose to greet her, and Frances felt as though she had received a body blow as the man turned to smile at her.

'Hello, Frances,' he greeted her. 'Thank goodness I've found you at last. Your father told me your new address here on the island.'

'Lionel!' she whispered. 'Lionel Wright.'

To Rory, looking on, it looked as though a light had been extinguished. Did she love Paul Denham so much that her disappointment would show so keenly? Frances had gone paper white and all the old misery had come back into her eyes. How she hated meeting people who reminded her of the past. She was even worse than she had been, when the sympathy of friends had made him want to scream.

'I'm staying in Douglas,' Lionel was telling her. 'I can't tell you how . . . how lovely it is to see you again. I hope I'll see a lot of you while I'm here.'

'I start a new job tomorrow,' she told him. 'I won't have much free time.'

'If I'd known, I could have been here a month ago,' said Lionel Wright, chagrined. 'I wrote, you know . . . several times.'

'You'll be free in the evenings, though,' put in Rory.

'I shall be tired. I . . . I shall have to get used to the job.' She stood up. 'I'm very tired now, I'm afraid. I . . . I'm sorry. Amy and I have had rather a strenuous day. I hope you don't mind if I just go upstairs now.'

She was gone, and Rory looked at Lionel Wright uncomfortably.

'Frances hasn't been good at meeting old friends since . . . since the accident. Sorry about that, Lionel. She'll be O.K. by tomorrow.'

'At least I can come out and talk to you,' said Lionel easily, 'until she gets

178

used to me again. I was . . . er . . . very fond of . . . of you both, in the old days. I was sorry about . . . '

'About my scar,' said Rory frankly. 'I've learned to talk about it, and ignore it too, now. One of my friends here soon put it into perspective for me.'

'And your father tells me you're writing now?'

Rory's eyes kindled with interest as he talked on his own subject to Lionel, while Deborah served tea. She was puzzled by Frances, but a look at Amy had reassured her. A day out in sunshine and fresh air had drained both of them of energy.

'I hope I may come again,' said Lionel to her, courteously, when eventually he rose to go. Frances hadn't come back downstairs, even after a short rest, as Rory had predicted.

'But of course, if Rory and Frances wish it. It's their home.'

'Sure you can come again,' said Rory. 'Frances will soon get used to her job, and she'll be panting to go out and enjoy herself, and forget all about office routine for a while. I expect it will be my turn next, if I can land a job on a newspaper, and manage to talk Dad round! He wants me to go to university and get a degree in English.'

'Nothing wrong in that,' said Lionel, smiling. 'See you tomorrow then.'

He turned, and Deborah was conscious of the fact that he was a very good-looking man. He was older than she had supposed at first; then she remembered Mark telling her about him, and how he had coached Frances at tennis. Mark must have asked him to call, knowing her to be worried about Frances' attitude to herself. He must have thought that Lionel Wright would give her something else to think about.

But it seemed to Deborah that it wasn't likely to be an old friend such as Lionel who could bring real happiness to Frances. She suspected that only one person could do that . . . Paul Denham.

★ ★ ★

Frances lay awake, wondering what she should do, the nightmare of guilt and fear washing over her again. Lionel Wright was the last person she ever wanted to see again, and for a while her heart cried out against her father for telling Lionel where to find her.

Then reason returned, and she reminded herself that Mark had no idea that she had been so foolish as to believe herself in love with Lionel, and to want to marry him before telling either of their parents.

She could hardly remember the child she had been then, her head full of dreams and romance, and so flattered because an older man wanted her, and had proposed marriage. She had not been ashamed of that love. She had been proud of Lionel and eager to marry him, but some sixth sense had told her that if even a whisper of how they felt reached the ears of their parents, then they would do all they could to separate them.

Lionel had agreed with her, and it

was his suggestion that they run away together. One was allowed to marry at sixteen in Scotland, Lionel had explained, so there would be no problem over that. He would arrange everything, and she trusted him implicitly.

In those days he had been very handsome and athletic. He dressed well because of his job, and she had been so proud to be seen with him. It was only later that she had wondered a little, wondered why he had preferred the child she had been then to a more mature woman. Then she remembered that he had already been let down once by an older girl. He wanted someone trustworthy, and she had vowed to herself that she would never let him down.

But because Lionel was so much older, she had felt unable to confide in Rory, except to tell him she was in love and going to be married. He had looked at her incredulously.

'You can't be serious! You mean,

you're running away? But *why*, Frances?'

'Because they'll stop us, that's why.'

'Then who is he, for heaven's sake? He must be awful, or something, when you're ashamed of him . . . '

'I'm not ashamed of him,' she had cried, her eyes bright with a mixture of tears and excitement. 'It's just that he's older than I am. They'll say he's too old and I'm too young, and age doesn't matter a bit. They'll spoil it all for us. Only . . . I couldn't go without telling you, Rory. Promise you won't tell. At least, not till after I've gone.'

She had been too excited to notice that Rory promised nothing. She had expected him to be on her side, but it had obviously worried him enough to go off to one of her mother's committee meetings and rake her out.

She had been waiting for Lionel outside the station, and he had witnessed the accident on his way to meet her, so that her dreamlike happiness had turned into a nightmare of fear and bewilderment.

She had seen the shock on his face when he arrived, and for a little while he had been unable to tell her, even going as far as to buy the tickets. But the shock had made him feel ill, and as they made for their train, he had faltered. She remembered her own panic that he had become suddenly ill, then the sense of numbed shock when he had blurted out the cause of it all.

Lionel had taken her to the hospital. Her father had been there beside her, then they had sat by Rory's bedside while he mumbled things incomprehensible to Mark, but which she understood with a growing sense of horror. Her mother's one thought had been to stop her. Rory had told her, after all. For a while Frances had wanted to pour out the whole story to her father, but she could find no words, and dimly she realised that it would only make things worse, not better.

She had seen Lionel only once more,

telling him that it was all over between them. He hadn't understood in the least.

'Surely you don't blame me,' he said, holding her tightly, though she pushed him away with an odd sense of revulsion.

She didn't blame him. She could only blame herself. She had agreed to marry Lionel, and to her a promise was a binding thing, even more binding in their case when he had already been let down by someone else. But she had still asked him to be free of that promise.

'This would always be between us,' she told him. 'You must see that, Lionel.'

'I see that you think it would at the moment,' he agreed, 'but later . . . '

'I can't imagine things will ever change.'

'Give it time, Frances darling.'

'No, Lionel. It's finished. A good clean break will be best, so I . . . I don't want ever to see you again.'

'But that's ridiculous!'

'No. It's the only way. You would just remind me . . . we would remind each other of all this horror. Have you seen Rory, too? They don't know that we won't lose him, as well as Mother. If we do, I . . . I'll never get over it. Never!'

He had gone to London, his eyes brooding with disappointment and she had not answered his letters. As time went by she could only think about him with revulsion. He was part of her life that she wanted to forget, and, as Rory got better and came home, it was she who suffered most every time she looked at the scar on his face.

She was terrified Lionel would keep trying to see her, until Rory saw that he must get her away from Glasgow, and took it upon himself to ask Mark for somewhere quiet where they could rest for a while. It would suit him very well, too, since he was beginning to dread so much sympathy.

'I don't want to see anybody,' he told

his father, and Mark had understood with regard to Rory, though he would not have understood if it had been only for Frances. As it was, he was doubtful about having her cut herself off from her friends, as well as Rory.

'We don't really want our friends to bother about us at the moment, Daddy,' she had pleaded, 'so please don't tell *anyone* where we've gone.'

'All right, if that's what you want,' Mark had agreed with a sigh.

But obviously Mark hadn't regarded Lionel in the same light as the other young people they knew. And now he was back and obviously wanting to see her again, and no doubt also wanting to pick up old threads.

Frances felt the old raw wounds beginning to hurt again. She didn't want Lionel. She didn't want to hear what he had to say, and she didn't want anyone to know what had happened between them. Most of all, she didn't want Rory to know that it had been Lionel she had wanted to marry.

Yet she would have to try to act normally with him, or Rory would suspect. Somehow it had been bearable when no one else knew but herself, but now . . . now she just wanted to lie down and cover her head with pillows. She had thought she could tell Paul, but now that she had seen Lionel again, she could not even tell Paul.

'He's old,' she thought, 'older than Debbie. He's nearly old enough to be my father.'

It was with some relief that she remembered her new job, and never would they have a more conscientious office worker, she vowed. She must put all her time and energy into that, and somehow persuade Lionel to go away.

But he wasn't so easy to persuade, she remembered. There was something clinging about Lionel, and she had never really felt free of him over the past two years.

She woke up, heavy-eyed, next morning while Deborah brought her a cup of tea and a lot of sympathy.

'Too excited to sleep, I bet,' she said, with a smile. 'Never mind, I'll run a bath for you, and it will freshen you up. You'll soon get used to being a working girl.'

9

For Frances, the first day in her new job was a confusing experience. Worried as she had been by Lionel Wright, she found her concentration lessened, and had to be shown several times before she took it in. To balance this however, she was full of determination to do well, and her boss nodded approval several times over her willingness to take endless trouble.

In fact, it was later than she had expected before she finally left her new office to head for home, hoping to catch a glimpse of June Carlie, who had sought her out for a quick snack at lunch-time.

But it was Lionel who stepped forward as soon as she appeared in the street, and Frances hesitated, then waited for him to come up to her. It was bound to happen, she thought tiredly. She would have to straighten things out with Lionel sooner or later, and make him believe she had not changed her mind and was willing to take up the old threads again.

'I've been waiting for you,' he greeted her. 'What time does that office of yours close? They must be antiquated.'

'They aren't at all antiquated. Some people *like* to finish their jobs before they just down tools and leave.'

'I wouldn't have thought you'd be one of them,' Lionel said teasingly, and took her arm with all the old familiarity. 'You look beautiful, Frances. I always thought you beautiful, and I knew you'd be even lovelier as you grew older. I can see now that I was right.'

'No, Lionel,' she protested.

'No?'

'No. I mean, please don't pay me any compliments. I . . . I don't want to hear them any more.'

'Oh, but surely, after two years, Fran. Two years! Isn't that long enough to have forgotten all . . . all that happened?

191

I understood then. Of course I did, otherwise I'd never have lost touch with you. But I knew I would wait, until you felt better . . . Look, darling, we'll go in here for a meal. I've told your nice Mrs Lacey that I'll be taking you out, and she thought that an excellent idea.'

'I don't want to go.'

Frances was tired. All she wanted was to get home and kick her shoes off, and let Deborah fuss over her a little. Rory, too, would be interested, and Amy would want a warm hug before she went off to sleep.

She was realising more each day how much she had come to love her new home, and she was certainly going to do nothing which would put her in danger of losing it. Somehow she must get rid of Lionel.

Reluctantly she allowed him to lead her into the hotel where he had booked a table for both of them. There was no use arguing in the street, and they couldn't talk at home. She didn't feel like eating very much, but she sat down at a small secluded table after having a wash to freshen herself up, and looked at Lionel, almost as though seeing him for the first time.

'Well?' he asked, laughing. 'Surely I can't have changed all that much!'

'No.' Her eyes were serious. 'Perhaps not a lot, Lionel, but I have. I'm not at all the same girl I was at sixteen . . . '

'That makes it all the more exciting,' he told her, leaning forward. 'You're even more attractive . . . '

'I was only a child, Lionel. Couldn't you have seen that?'

'*You* didn't think so. You'd have been ready to scratch my eyes out if I'd suggested such a thing. You were absolutely sure of yourself, Frances, so don't try telling me I was baby-snatching, because you were no baby.'

But she had been, thought Frances. Underneath all that pretence, she had been young, and frightened sometimes. That was why she had clung to Lionel, feeling he was so much older, and could think and plan for both of them. So often she had gone home with worries and problems, but no one was there to listen to them, and reassure her. Not even Rory most times, though he was always willing to listen even if he couldn't give her the help she needed.

'But surely you see we could never take up the threads again, Lionel. Everything changed. It all happened . . . Mummy . . . the accident . . . because she was desperate to stop us going away and getting married. You knew that. I told you so at the time. Even . . . even if I had continued to love you, it would always have been between us.'

'Only if we let it, Frances. You make too much of it, darling.'

The words were familiar to her. It was what Rory had said when he urged her to contact Paul again.

The thought of Paul brought pain. How could she ever be anything to Paul, with Lionel Wright so determined to be back in her life? If she was very firm and told him to go away, he probably would, but he would always drift back again.

'I'm tired, Lionel,' she told him, and this he did accept. 'I don't really want to discuss it. I can only tell you that it would have been a mistake two years ago. I was saved from making that mistake, but at terrible expense. It . . . it would have brought you unhappiness, too, Lionel. I know it would.'

'That's not true, darling. We would have been happy . . . '

'Please! Just leave me alone to live my own life.'

Lionel's eyes glittered as he said softly,

'You forget, my love, it's my life, too. I've been trying to find you, you know, and it was a bit of luck contacting your father. *He* didn't appear to be so unwelcoming. Or Rory.'

'They don't know,' she cut in quickly. 'I never told them who you were. You know we planned to tell them later.'

'So . . . ' He sat back, his eyes suddenly shrewd. 'So they don't know I was almost in the family. I wondered about that.'

'Please don't tell them, Lionel. Please. I ... I'd rather they didn't know. Rory knew I was going away, but that's all. You know I had to tell him, but I never told him who it was, and Daddy never knew anything about it.'

'I see. Well, darling, I make no promises. But I'm not leaving so easily. I think you need time to get used to having me around again. Think of all the good times, how you used to run to me with all your little problems. But I intend to win you all over again. But for chance ... fate, if you like ... you'd have been my wife for the past two years and I'm not giving that up so easily. So eat something, for goodness' sake. You've picked at your food all evening.'

'I'm not hungry.'

'I don't pay for good meals to have them wasted.'

'Then eat it yourself. I'm going home, Lionel. Goodnight.'

'Au revoir, you mean. All right, I'll take you home, if that's what you want.'

'I *don't* belong to you. Just don't bother me, that's all.'

'No bother, darling. No bother at all.'

★ ★ ★

'I hope that job you've found for Frances isn't too much for her.'

Rory looked at June, his eyes troubled.

'She should be able to do it on her head. Though I must admit she looked as though she *were* doing it on her head.'

June got up to come over and sit beside him on the settee, gathering together the pages of a manuscript which she had been reading.

'This isn't as good as usual, Rory. I don't think you'll sell it.'

'Thanks for the encouragement.'

'Don't you know what's wrong with her, Rory? It may not be the job.'

'It could be Paul Denham. I rather

think she fell for him a bit while he was home.'

'Hm.' June sat back and hugged her arms thoughtfully. 'Shouldn't be any problem there. I rather think our Paul found her attractive, too.'

Rory shot her a sideways glance.

'And you, June? Do you find Paul attractive?'

She stared at him, surprised.

'Not more so than anyone else. Why? Not jealous, are you?'

'No, but I think Frances was.'

'You're joking!'

'Cross my heart. She saw you taking tender farewell of him the evening before he left for Manchester.'

June's brows wrinkled.

'His last evening,' she said, after a while. 'I remember. Hang it all, Rory, I've known Paul all my life. He's as much to me as . . . as that old friend of yours . . .'

'Lionel Wright.'

'Yes . . . is to you and Frances.' Her eyes grew reflective. 'Though I must say, I find your Lionel a bit wet.'

'A bit wet! He's an athlete, June, practically a professional at tennis. He used to coach Frances until she was far better than average.'

'I'm not talking about his looks, darling. He's like a smoothie-type film star . . . till you look a bit closer. There's just something . . . Oh, I don't know.'

'No, go on. Try telling me.'

Rory was beginning to put great dependence on June's judgement.

'I can't,' she laughed. 'Just imagination. He's older than we are, anyway. If he were younger, I'd suspect he was after Frances, but he's at least twice her age, and I don't think she finds him attractive.'

'I shouldn't think so either,' laughed Rory. 'Poor old Lionel!'

'Why poor?'

'Oh, I don't know. Because he always seemed to be on the fringe of things, I suppose. Neither his own generation, nor ours.'

They were silent for a while, then Rory spoke again.

'June, give Frances the hint, will you? About Paul, I mean. It might help. You see, she . . . well, she rather fell for someone two years ago, only it all petered out when we had the accident. Now I think she's ashamed of that, in the past, and she keeps heading Paul off.'

'But not so far off as to be jealous of other girls,' said June dryly.

'We are all weak flesh,' Rory intoned. 'Maybe the Nesbits are weaker than most.'

Her golden-tipped eyelashes veiled her eyes and she turned away a little.

'Poor old Nesbits! Never mind, Rory, my dear. I'll see Frances. If she's back to biting my nose off for my pains, I shall slap her, I promise you.'

Rory chuckled.

'And I hope you'll be suitably chastened when I get paid for this short story.'

'No pay for that one, old lad. Back to

the drawing board, and start again. How's the book?'

'No pay for that either,' said Rory, suddenly gloomy. 'Sometimes I feel I'm wasting my time.'

'Now I shall have to slap *you*,' she promised, turning towards him with a swirl of her pleated skirt. For a moment there was no banter in Rory as he looked at her, then he turned away and June picked up her bag.

'No slipping back, Rory,' she said quietly. 'It isn't half as bad as you think.'

He didn't accompany her to the door, but watched her tall young figure as she ran lightly down the path and out of the gate, with a quick wave of her hand. And there were depths in Rory's eyes, which she hadn't seen.

'Was that June?' asked Deborah, coming in the back door, and catching a glimpse of her going out of the gate. Amy was helping her to carry a basket of vegetables.

'Yes,' said Rory briefly. 'Frances is

still out with old Lionel. She said they'd be back for tea.'

He sat down again on the settee, and picked up his manuscript.

'Deborah! What do you think of Lionel?'

She glanced at him, but he was thumbing over the manuscript.

'He . . . I don't really know him,' she hedged.

'Don't wriggle out of it, as June might say.'

'In what way, then? He seems a harmless sort of person.'

'A bit wet?'

Deborah paused, then her eyes met Rory's, and they both laughed.

'Yes, maybe he's a bit wet.'

'I want June to tackle Frances about that job of hers. She puts hours into it, and I think she works all night, too, in her dreams. She's so determined to be brisk and efficient, that she seems to be living on her nerves to do it.'

'It's her first job,' said Deborah. 'She wants to take it seriously.'

'No, there's more to it than that.'

Deborah nodded. She knew this was true, but she'd been so hoping that Frances was at last beginning to settle, that she had been prepared to put the blinkers on.

'Can I set the table for Rory and Frances and you and me?' asked Amy hopefully.

She didn't want Lionel, though the natural good manners which were in her, even as a child, kept her from saying so. She didn't have to, thought Deborah with a sigh. Amy only had to look.

'No,' she said firmly. 'You set it for five. Mr Wright will be here, too.'

'Frances doesn't like him,' said Amy.

'Now that's enough,' her mother said sharply.

'Well, she doesn't. She likes me a lot better.'

Deborah considered her. Was Amy being shrewd, or was she just a little bit jealous? Fervently she wished Mark home again, even for a short weekend.

Pressure of business had kept him in Glasgow over the past two weeks, and it seemed a long time since he had been here. There was little likelihood of him arriving the following morning either, as he usually telephoned to say he was coming.

Deborah took a firm hold of herself. She was allowing herself to be swept more and more into Mark Nesbit's life, like a leaf bobbing on the water, being swept up and entangled in a branch.

Gradually she was beginning to look on the Nesbits as her own family, and saw that Amy, too, loved all of them. She had grown close to Rory, and for a while she had felt a new relationship between herself and Frances, as though the girl was glad to be home any time she had been away.

Recently, though, she had grown concerned about her, again, and sometimes impatient. Frances was so moody and difficult, that she often felt she would wash her hands of her . . . let her stew in her own juice, as June had put it. Then she would catch the girl in an unguarded moment, and feel her heart go out to her. Frances' vivid blue eyes looked haunted with the battle she was fighting inside herself. It was then that Deborah would begin to feel that she had imagined any point of contact between them, because if there had been, surely Frances would have come to her for help, even in an oblique way. Surely she would know that she was always there, waiting to give whatever help and encouragement she could.

* * *

The following morning Deborah was in by herself, when there was a familiar step at the back door, and when she turned and saw Mark in the doorway, surprise tore away her normal defences, and she stood there with her heart in her eyes.

'Mark!'

A moment later she was in his arms,

being held as though he would never let her go.

'Deborah! Darling, I'm so glad to be home.'

'Oh, Mark! What a wonderful thing to say.'

'You don't know how wonderful it is to feel one has a home . . . and you waiting for me. I'd never dared hope you would . . . Deborah, you *are* glad to see me? I . . . I didn't make a mistake? You do care for me a little?'

She drew back, suddenly shy.

'I . . . '

'It means everything to me, you see. I think I fell in love with you from the first, but I never thought . . . I'm older than you, Deborah.'

She was shaking her head.

'I'm not a young girl, Mark. I'm a widow, with a young daughter.'

'Then you'd care enough to marry me?'

This time she drew back.

'Please . . . let's just get used to . . . to caring for one another. There are more people to be considered than just the two of us. I couldn't marry you unless Rory and Frances wanted it, too.'

'They'll want to lead their own lives, Deborah. I think we're entitled to our happiness as well.'

Deborah nodded, but her eyes were still troubled.

'I'd still like it to be just us for a little while. Please, Mark . . . '

Again he held her close.

'All right, darling. But I shan't be able to hide my happiness. They'll guess anyway. What about Amy?'

'No problem with Amy.'

'Thank goodness for that!'

A small sound caught Deborah's ear and she turned quickly.

'What's that? Someone's home, Mark. I heard the hall door.'

She hurried through the lounge and opened the door into the hall. Frances was mounting the stairs, and she turned swiftly as Deborah opened the door, her face white and strained.

'Oh, it's you, Frances! Your father has come . . . '

'Yes, I know. Hello, Daddy. Excuse me, but I must go upstairs.'

Deborah turned to Mark as they heard the door of Frances' room closing.

'Do you think she heard, Mark? Or saw anything? Do you think she's upset? She's been worrying about things again, just lately.'

'What if she did see?' asked Mark. 'She has to know some time.'

'But if it hurts her. Mark, I think the children keep remembering their mother. I think they must have loved Una very much.'

'Of course they did. I loved her, too, and I would hope you loved Patrick. We won't ever forget either of them, or fail to think of them with gratitude for what we had. But there are many years ahead of us, Deborah. We're condemning each other to a long lonely life if we set too much store by what Frances feels. I'm sure Una would be happy for me to have found you.'

But Deborah refused to set aside all her reservations.

'I think they'll have to get used to the idea gently, Mark. It would make all the difference to the years ahead. I refuse to be an unwanted stepmother.'

'I hope you won't refuse to be a very much wanted wife,' said Mark quietly. 'I think we pander to our children far too much.'

'Right now I'd better start pandering to you, Mark. You must be awfully hungry by now. I'll soon have a meal on the table.'

'We ought to have champagne. I still feel like celebrating!'

Deborah laughed, but inside she was rather uneasy. She hoped, indeed, that they did have something to celebrate. Then, as she looked again at Mark, she could only feel the comfort of having him nearby. She loved him, and she wanted him. That was enough for now.

★   ★   ★

Frances lay face downwards on her bed, having pulled the curtains to keep out the sunlight. Her head ached and she felt more tired than she had ever done in her life. It was as though she was too tired to think any more, yet she must think if she was going to carry on with her life, trying to live through each day normally.

She had tried to make Lionel Wright see that she didn't want him any more, and to ask him to go away and never see her again, but there was still two weeks of his holiday to run. Could she stick it out for two whole weeks? she wondered. Without making such a strong stand that her whole family would know that she had once before made promises to Lionel which she hadn't been able to keep? She had promised that she would always love him, and that she would marry him against all opposition. She had been brought up to believe that one must always keep one's promise, but she hadn't kept hers, and now Lionel was holding her to ransom, if morally. Now she had learned that he had remained steadfast and wanted her more than ever, whereas she only wanted to be free of every promise she had ever made to him.

Only how could she free herself? How could she make him see that she would never love him again? He just went on being patient with her, and that, she found, was much worse than masterful opposition. Hitting one's head against a brick wall reminded one that the wall was there. But with Lionel it was more like trying to get hold of a piece of quicksilver, or groping to catch a wall of mist. There was just nothing to take hold of, yet every free moment found him waiting for her with quiet good humour and patience. However tired she felt, he told her she looked beautiful and she had to bring all her wiles to bear on being free of him, even for a little while. It was like being smothered with cotton wool.

'I can't stand it for another two

weeks,' she said aloud, and rested her hot forehead on her arms. Even if he did go away, she would never know the minute he would return. Already she was making too many stupid mistakes in her new job, and Miss Haley, who was in charge of the office, had warned her that she must be replaced if she didn't do better.

'You young girls don't get enough rest,' she told Frances, looking at her pale face. 'You can't do your work properly throughout the day, and enjoy yourself half the night. It means that your mind is much too befogged for concentration. Just bear that in mind, Miss Nesbit. You'll have to re-plan your evenings if you're going to be any help to us in this office. In fact, we're better with no one than a girl who is a hindrance. Now, please try to find that file again. You must have put it *somewhere.*'

Frances had known better than to make excuses, but if she still had the job in another week, it would be a miracle.

And June would want to know why.

Frances had begun to develop a respect for June. The other girl did a lot of straight talking, but you knew where you were with her. She had made Frances blush with a few pointed remarks about her friendship with Paul, and how easy it is to jump to conclusions.

Yet if she was no longer jealous of June because of Paul, it still solved nothing.

Frances knew she would have to do something. But what? She tried to look into the future, but it became a mere jumble of thoughts, even as she listened to the normally comforting sounds of the table being set for a meal.

She must get away again, she thought, where she could put things into proper perspective. She couldn't sit in with her family and behave normally when she couldn't concentrate on even normal conversation.

There was a light knock on the door, and Amy poked her head in.

'Mummy says it's lunch-time. She'll be sounding the gong in a minute. Will you be ready, Frances?'

She sat up and tried to smile at the child.

'I ... I'm not awfully hungry, darling.'

'It's only ham and salad, though Mummy plans something special for this evening. I heard her say so.'

'Oh.'

'So you'd better come, Frances. Shall I take your hand? Aren't you feeling well?'

'My head aches, that's all. But don't tell anyone. It's a secret between you and me.'

'A secret,' Amy agreed.

She rose from the bed and took the little girl's hand, feeling that the only way to avoid attention from the others was to act as normally as possible.

'Didn't you get your letter, dear?' asked Deborah, appearing with it from where it had been lying on the hall table.

'Thank you,' said Frances quietly, slipping it into her pocket. It was from Paul, but again she felt that his letters were bitter-sweet. He wrote to her, as to a friend, with brisk friendliness so that she felt that was how he pictured her, as only a friend.

During the meal, Frances allowed her father and Deborah to do all the talking. They both looked animated, but she was too wrapped up in her own affairs to notice anything unusual, and after lunch she again excused herself, saying she had letters to write.

'Or to read!' thought Deborah.

She looked at Frances rather uneasily now and again. Had the girl now guessed about herself and Mark? There had been suspicions once before, and she had felt hurt and angry, but now it seemed that Frances had seen further than she had herself.

She felt disappointed that she had not grown closer to Frances, and she had felt they were becoming friends, then the girl had put up the barriers again. It was impossible for her to guess how she would feel about having Deborah for a stepmother, but she feared that it would not be well received. Yet Mark was insisting that the children be told.

'They have to know some time,' he pointed out. 'I just don't see the sense in putting it off.'

But would that shatter the small amount of contact she had with Frances? Deborah just couldn't decide, and her new happiness in her love for Mark kept smothering her worries, so that she looked lovely in the brightness of her happiness. Mark hardly took his eyes from her, and if Frances had not been so worried, there would have been no need to break the news to her that they hoped to marry.

But instead she was excusing herself as soon as she could, and going back upstairs.

Later it was again Rory who received her confidence, in the form of a small note. They had been too close to each other over the years for her to leave him without a word.

'This time I'm running from Lionel,' she wrote, 'not with him. How ironic can you get!'

But Rory had spent the day with new friends he had made from Ramsay, and it was late when he got home. By that time Frances had slipped out of the house with a small weekend case, and this time no one saw her go. Mark and Deborah were too busy making plans of their own, and Amy was playing with one of her friends.

Frances took a bus to Douglas, then out to Ronaldsway where she was lucky enough to get a seat on a plane for Manchester.

Barely an hour later, she felt as though she was in another world.

10

Rory stared at the letter, having to read it several times before he took it all in. Frances had asked him to say nothing to her father about Lionel, reminding Rory that she was old enough now to stand on her own feet, and to make decisions for herself. Circumstances were different from the last time she had asked him to keep a secret.

She would get a job, and would be perfectly all right, though she had carefully avoided giving any hint of where she intended to look for that job. Could she have gone back to Glasgow? he wondered, biting his lip. To Aunt Marion? . . . though Frances had never been close to Aunt Marion. Or would she make for London? No, not London. Lionel Wright would be going back there.

Lionel Wright . . . Lionel Wright!

Rory read the letter again, slow anger beginning to burn. Surely Frances could never have fallen for a creep like Lionel! Already Rory had forgotten his own liking for the man, and now he felt he had never been able to understand her enthusiasm for Lionel, and put it down to his ability to play games with the speed and certainty which amount almost to professional standard.

He had always been good-looking, with a strong athletic body, but Rory decided, again, that there ended Lionel Wright. There was no depth to him at all. People had wondered why he had never married but it had been no puzzle to Rory, who believed that he would bore any girl of his own generation to death before he could get close enough to pop the question! He could only impress a very young girl like Frances, thought Rory, his anger growing, before she had developed enough sense to see through him. And he had been irresponsible enough to want her to run away with him!

Rory began to see why Frances had kept the affair hidden. There would certainly have been the mother and father of all rows if their parents had got to hear of it, and the Wrights would not have liked it any better. Frances would have been young enough to be Lionel's daughter.

And now he had come into her life, and was bothering her again, refusing to take no for an answer. Rory read again all Frances had to say, and he could understand what she meant perfectly.

'He's like a handful of mist,' she wrote, 'only a mist which won't go away altogether. He's always there, hovering around, but when I try to get hold of him to make him see reason, then he just drifts about, then settles back down again. I just can't get rid of him, Rory. Sometimes I think I never will, so I'm running out. Don't tell Daddy . . . I'd be so ashamed.

'I feel so guilty, because I *did* promise Lionel I would always love him, and I swore I'd never change, but I have, Rory. I don't think I could ever really have loved him at all, though it seemed real enough at the time.'

Rory's eyebrows drew together as he read on. He was to tell Lionel, when he called, that Frances had gone to stay with friends.

'He'll soon go back home when he realises I'm not on the island.'

Rory sat back, the scar suddenly livid again on his face. Poor Frances! She had certainly got herself into a state, if she thought that was all he was going to do about it. He was being asked to show Lionel the door, politely, but in such a way that he would imagine it would always remain open to him, open and welcome.

Well, he was no 'handful of mist' to Rory. He would deal with Lionel Wright, if it was the last thing he did. Indirectly the man was responsible for the loss of his mother, and his long weeks in hospital, not to mention the results he would carry around all his life. If he hadn't encouraged Frances . . .

Rory had to leap off the bed and walk up and down to control his anger, then reason began to take over, and again he felt concern for Frances. She hadn't very much money, he was sure, and she seemed very young and vulnerable to be away on her own like that. But surely she would have the sense to go to someone she knew, even for a little while.

It was late, but Rory felt he could not sleep without a glass of hot milk or something. It was too late now to do anything about Frances. The others must have left her alone, feeling she had locked her door in order to rest, but now Rory looked at the key which had been left in the envelope. Should he give it to Deborah tonight? Should he knock on her door to see if she was still awake, or leave it all till morning?

The decision was taken out of his hands when he went quietly downstairs to the kitchen, because Deborah was still sitting there, looking pensive but at peace, in the large old chair in the corner of the kitchen.

'Rory!' she cried, jumping up. 'I thought you were asleep, my dear. I was just . . . just sorting out a few things for the morning.'

'Oh.' He looked embarrassed.

'What's the matter?' she asked gently. 'Couldn't you sleep? Frances seems to be off colour, too. She went to bed very early, and asked not to be disturbed.'

'She . . . she isn't in bed,' he said, unable to keep it to himself any longer. 'She's gone.'

'Gone!'

'Yes. That's why . . . she hasn't been down for tea or anything. She'd locked her door, to make you think she was lying down. Here's the key.'

He produced it from his pocket and handed it to her.

'But why? Why?'

This time Rory could not find the words to tell her the truth. He couldn't do that without betraying Frances' confidence, so he could only turn away, his cheeks flaming.

'I think . . . she says she'd just like to stand on her own feet for a while. She's old enough . . . '

'Oh, Rory! She's such a young eighteen!'

'Well, yes . . . well, but she thinks she's old enough. She'll write when she's settled. I . . . perhaps I could tell Father in the morning. He's only got tomorrow, hasn't he?'

'No. I think he might prefer to be told tonight,' said Deborah firmly.

'Then I'd better do it,' said Rory hurriedly. 'If he's awfully fast asleep, do you think . . . ?'

Mark had taken a sleeping pill, and reluctantly Deborah agreed to leave it till the morning, her heart softened by the sight of Mark sleeping so soundly. He looked young and rather vulnerable in deep sleep, and she and Rory tiptoed back out of his bedroom.

'I suppose it can't make much difference now,' she conceded. 'If she was catching a plane, she just won't be on the island and there won't be a plane till morning. Is there *no* clue as to where she has gone?'

'None at all,' said Rory, shaking his head.

He looked very tired, the scar almost purple against the whiteness of his face, and Deborah put a hand gently on his arm.

'Go to bed, dear. I'll bring you a hot drink and we'll try to get you some sleep.'

But it was Deborah who lay awake for a long time, her happiness in shreds. So Frances *had* heard. She knew that her father now contemplated putting someone in her mother's place, and the young girl couldn't bear the thought of it.

Rather than stay to be given this news, she had stolen away when no one was around to see, and gone to be by herself for a while.

Only she was so young, thought Deborah wretchedly, and her imagination worked over time as she thought of all the things which could happen to a young girl on her own, and probably not feeling at all well because of her unhappiness.

It was a very long time before Deborah fell asleep.

★ ★ ★

Her new, exciting happiness hadn't lasted long, thought Deborah next morning, as she and Mark faced each other like strangers. It was as though there was no point of contact between them, and he could not see her point of view.

Rory hadn't come downstairs, having no doubt lain awake, as she had, for a long time, then sleeping too late in the morning.

'Leave him,' she pleaded with Mark when he rose from the breakfast table and would have gone straight up to Rory's room, after she had broken the news about Frances. 'Do leave him a little longer, Mark. He was so tired last night.'

'I'd like to know what's been going on between them,' said Mark, upset by the news, and growing angry. 'I'd like to know why she felt the need to rush off like this, without saying where she was going, or telling anyone a thing about it. *And* on top of finding a job for herself. Surely she's got sense enough to know we would be worried about her. It's high time she stopped throwing all these tantrums, for whatever reason, and began to remember the rest of us. Hasn't she got any consideration at all?'

'Mark . . . ' Deborah's voice trembled a little with nerves. 'Mark, can't you see why she's gone?'

'Should I? What is there in this house which is so obviously abhorrent to my daughter that she must cut and run? Have I been cruel or unjust to her in any way? Is it cruel to look after her, and try to pander to her every whim? Because that's just what did happen, and I can see now that it was a gross mistake. She should . . . '

'No! No, it isn't you, Mark. Don't

you see? It's me!'

'You! Why, you've been nothing but the soul of goodness.'

'*Us* then. Us, my dear. Frances has . . . has guessed, you see. That's what she's running away from.'

Mark stopped walking up and down and turned to stare at her.

'I don't believe it. Frances would never run away like that if she disapproved of the fact that we wanted to marry. She'd come right out and say so . . . try to fight, if you like. She would put her oar in, even if it was none of her business.'

'But, Mark, she saw us. I'm sure she did. Or heard us, maybe. Once before she said something . . . something which made me wonder at the time if she didn't suspect such a thing. Don't you remember? It was ages ago, but I did tell you, at the time.'

'I think you're imagining more than is there.'

'No, I'm sure I'm not. You see, Frances must have cared even more for her mother than anyone could realise. The evidence is all there. I've never seen a girl so upset by losing her mother that her whole life seems to have been changed. I . . . I could sense it, every time I talked to her. A girl like that isn't going to take lightly to having someone else in her mother's place.'

Mark had stopped pacing, and now he came to sit beside Deborah on the settee.

'I'll find her,' he said, 'and bring her home again, then we can have it out with her . . . bring it all into the open. Things can't be left in the air like this. You're as good as saying that . . . that you can't marry me because Frances wouldn't like it. Am I right?'

His face was white and she could feel the tension in him. She nodded.

'You wouldn't want it either, if it was going to make your only daughter so unhappy. You're only angry with her now because you're worried about her, as I am. But I think you agree with me in your heart, don't you, Mark, that we can't take our happiness at the expense of hers.'

He was silent for a long time, then he took her hand.

'I know what you mean, and it's because you're the person you *are* that I do love you. Only you could put a young girl's happiness before your own. So many women would want to hold on to what was theirs, and leave everything else to take care of itself. I ... I suppose it's that quality in you which I recognised first. Yet it's that very quality which is losing you to me.'

His grip tightened and he pulled her to him closely, and she felt her heart swelling at the thought of the brief happiness they had shared. Somehow she had felt that because they did love one another, everything would turn out all right, but now the future was blank. She could see no life together for them ahead.

A smothered exclamation made her stiffen, and they turned to see Rory staring at them.

'Oh, lor'! I . . . I'm sorry,' he stammered. 'I . . . I was just going to get . . . '

'No, stay, Rory,' his father told him. 'You know now how I feel about Deborah. I don't expect it's any surprise to you. I had asked her to marry me, and she'd agreed, but things are different now that Frances has gone.'

'Different?'

'Yes. Deborah is sure Frances left home because she guessed about us, and is unhappy about it. She doesn't want to see Deborah in . . . in your mother's place. Is that really so, Rory? Would *you* feel that way?'

'Of course not!' cried Rory. 'I don't mind you and Debbie getting married. In fact, it would be smashing, nothing I'd like better.'

His young face was scarlet with embarrassment, however, and the older couple also felt awkward, feeling it could not be easy for him.

'But what about Frances?' asked

Deborah quietly. 'I *am* right, aren't I, Rory? She heard us talking or . . . or saw us . . . just as you did.'

'I think Frances would have stayed to express her views,' said Mark. 'She's very honest about things like that. If she didn't approve, she'd come right out with it, and say so.'

'But she may not want to hurt you, Mark,' put in Deborah. 'She may have *wanted* to express her views, but she'll be torn between love for her mother, or her mother's memory, and love for you. She's wise enough to see that you could be lonely, and would be happier married again, but she may not be able to face all that right now.' She appealed to Rory again. 'You know her better than I do. What do you think, my dear?'

Rory felt tongue-tied. Should he tell them about Lionel? But if he did, he would have to tell the whole story, of the part Lionel Wright had to play in the accident which killed his mother. And his father knew nothing about that!

How would Mark react if he was told all about it now? He would be ready to go to Lionel Wright with murder in his heart, doubly so because of Una, and now because of Frances. And Lionel was much more athletic than his father, even if no one could call Mark a weakling. If he went into a rage and struck Lionel, then the other man would probably defend himself, and Rory could not bear the thought of his father being hurt in any way. He would have to take care of Lionel himself.

Deborah watched the uncertainty on Rory's face, and the hesitation as he tried to speak once or twice, and drew her own conclusions.

'I don't think it was that entirely,' he told them.

'I'm sure of it. I . . . I think she just wants to feel grown up, to stand on her own feet for a while.'

'Without leaving an address?' asked Mark. 'She must know we wouldn't have objected if she wanted to try her wings. Only I'd like to know that she was off to a reasonably good start . . . '

'That isn't trying her wings,' broke in Rory. 'Maybe that's what she's running from. You'd have been away seeing to it that she had proper accommodation, and giving her an allowance etc. till she found a job. That isn't really making her feel her independence.'

'Is that *all* it is, Rory?' asked Deborah, 'that she wants to be independent?'

His face flamed.

'Yes,' he lied manfully. 'It's all right, really. You . . . it isn't you. Honest. She won't mind at all if you two get married.'

'I shall want to hear that from Frances,' Deborah said stubbornly. 'Don't you know where she is at all? Not even the faintest idea?'

This time Rory was on safer ground, and he relaxed.

'No. I haven't a clue.'

'Here's Lionel coming,' said his father, staring out of the window. 'He won't know where she's gone, will he?

She always used to confide in him.'

Deborah's eyes had still been on Rory's face, and she saw the sudden flash in the boy's eyes, as though the presence of Lionel was a shock to him. She was sure of it by the way Rory jumped to his feet, saying he couldn't stay, but he would see Lionel later.

'I'm meeting June,' he told them, 'and I've no time to get involved talking to Lionel Wright, but don't go asking him questions, Dad. If he knows anything, I'll get it out of him. I'll go and see him this afternoon.'

'Well, if you think that's the best way . . . '

'I do. If he knows anything, he might have had time to think by then and he'll tell me, so don't make things difficult. Let me handle it. There he is at the front door now, so I'll just slip out the back.'

'I'll let him in,' Deborah said.

Rory hurried away, zipping up his anorak against the fresh breezes from the sea. He couldn't face Lionel Wright at the moment, or the rage he felt within him would surely boil over. He would want to punch out at his handsome face, and then everyone would know. There would have been no point in his evasions to Mark.

He had lied when he told them that he had to see June, but now he felt the need to see her, and talk with her. When his world started to go wrong, she was the one to make everything seem normal again. A few words of good sound common sense, and everything came back into perspective.

Besides, she would have to know about Frances, and perhaps she could do something about her job, one of the things which had concerned Frances most.

* * *

It was late afternoon by the time Rory went along to the hotel where Lionel Wright was staying. He knew that Lionel liked having tea at that time, but

236

he had no clear idea as to how he was going to see Lionel on his own. He must first of all see him alone, then play it by ear, he decided, but when he asked for Lionel at Reception, the pretty young girl at the desk was apologetic.

'Oh dear, you've missed him. He checked out about two hours ago.'

'Oh.' Rory felt deflated. Somehow he just had not thought of such a thing. He knew Lionel Wright still planned to spend the remaining two weeks of his holiday on the island, and he had imagined that he would still be here during that time.

'Er . . . you mean he had to leave Douglas?' he asked.

'I'm afraid I don't know, but I think he was going to the airport.'

'Thank you.'

Rory left the hotel foyer, and made for the promenade, walking along rather aimlessly in much the same way as his father had done just a week or two before, trying to sort out his thoughts and emotions. He had been keyed up to have things out with Lionel, and now he felt angry and frustrated, chagrined with himself for somehow bungling things.

Nor had June helped! Somehow he had taken it for granted that she would be free when he called, but she was just on her way to watch go-kart racing with Michael Derby, another friend whom Rory liked quite a lot. Yet he had felt rather let down to see June going off arm in arm with Mike, and he assured himself that this was because he had wanted to talk to her so badly. He had always liked Mike, hadn't he? He shouldn't feel annoyed with him for taking June out.

Rory put up a hand to touch the scar on his cheek. June had made him believe that it didn't matter, but if he had fallen in love with . . . *if* he had . . . would it really have made no difference when he asked her to marry him?

Rory's heart told him that it would, and as he made his way home, his anger against Lionel increased with every minute. The accident might not exactly have ruined his life, but it had made it much more difficult. In many ways it was also making him grow up, and he thought, rather tiredly, of the further disappointments he had had recently with his writing. His articles were not good, but his fiction had been doing better and now he was wondering if it would not be a good idea to eat humble pie and ask his father to take him into the business. He didn't want university at all. He could keep on writing short stories, then books, in his spare time, and hope that one day he could earn enough to do it professionally.

And in the meantime, he would see to it that his father was not short-changed. He would be willing to learn all he could about the business, and do it to the best of his ability.

These thoughts had been working away vaguely in his mind for some time, and now he felt a new strength of purpose. There would be changes afoot if his father married Debbie. Wouldn't they have to live in Glasgow, and what would happen to the house here, on the island? If Frances succeeded in making a new life for herself on her own, then there would only be himself to consider.

But it was difficult to see Frances being happy merely through her own independence, and the worry of her whereabouts and how she might be faring, once again gnawed at Rory. Where was she? Suppose she got ill . . .

★ ★ ★

Rory returned home with his scar a tell-tale livid red, and Deborah saw immediately that he was upset.

'Have you been to see Lionel?' she asked, with concern, as she gave him tea.

'No. Yes, rather.' Rory frowned. 'He's gone. Deborah, what did you say to him? Only that Frances had gone?'

'Yes. He seemed awfully concerned

about her. But then he would be, wouldn't he? From what Mark says, Lionel has considered himself responsible for Frances for years. Dutch uncle, he said.'

'Dutch uncle!' repeated Rory bitterly, and Deborah shot a glance at him. What did that mean? She said nothing but her eyes were thoughtful as she prepared tea, then with some purpose she came through to sit beside him.

'Rory, is there something between you and Lionel Wright? Could it be that he has an idea where Frances has gone? If so, please tell me. I . . . I can't settle or feel happy till we know where she is.'

Rory bit his lip. Should he tell Deborah? Yet he couldn't ask her to respect his confidence. She would be bound to tell his father.

'Where's Dad?' he asked, and she did not answer for a moment, but regarded him even more alertly, her eyes shrewd.

'I take it there's something you don't want your father to know,' she said quietly. 'He's just taken Amy out for a moment, to buy sweets. They'll be back any time. But, Rory, if there's anything you know which will help, I do urge you to tell your father. Can't you think of any young friends in Glasgow to whom she could have gone?'

Rory shook his head.

'Your father has rung up all the people he can think of, while Lionel was here. Even your Aunt Marion, though he was very reluctant to worry her. I wondered about Paul Denham . . . if she might have gone to talk to him. Mark was going to ask Mrs Denham for Paul's telephone number.'

'Did you mention Paul while Lionel was here?' asked Rory quickly.

Deborah thought for a moment.

'Only in a casual way. Why?'

'Did you say that there . . . I mean, that they're just friends?'

She frowned.

'I only said she might have gone to Paul for advice, and when Lionel asked who he was, I told him that Paul was curate of a church in Manchester.'

'But not the name of the church?'

'No . . . yes. It came up later. I rather think I did tell him. Why?'

Rory's face was very red.

'It may mean nothing,' he said.

'I think you'd better tell me,' said Deborah.

'And I think you'd better tell both of us,' echoed Mark, as he came quietly through the door. 'Amy has brought a friend home,' he added to Deborah. 'They're in the garden. Now, Rory, out with it. I can see you're trying to hide something. I've seen that look on your face a few times over the years.'

Rory swallowed, then it was as though all his pent-up feelings over the past two years were released, and he began to talk, at first with difficulty, stammering and hesitating, then more easily as he told them about Frances, and how Una had found out about her wanting to marry an older man.

Mark's face was carved out of grey stone as he listened, and Deborah felt that part of her was withdrawing into a shell. This was the story of the family, before she had any part in it. She felt like an outsider, on the fringe of it all, though she held Rory's hand in sympathy even as she listened with horror to all they had gone through.

'I mean, it wouldn't happen now, Dad, but that was two years ago, and we were both young and stupid, Frances as well as I. We didn't see all that much of you and Mother . . . '

Mark's eyes grew dark with pain. That was true. How many times he had regretted it!

'I didn't know who it was Frances had been seeing. She said she would write and tell me later, when it would be too late to stop her. She was determined that she knew her own mind, you see. It was only since she ran away . . . now . . . that she's told me, in the note she left. It was Lionel Wright! Lionel!! I ask you.'

Mark jerked to his feet, striding up and down in a movement now familiar to Deborah, when he was upset. This time she could feel that he was fighting blind rage, though in Mark's heart it was all mixed up with guilt and remorse. He had not made a very good job of protecting and cherishing his family, had he?

Yet here he was, asking for a second chance with Deborah. She had been right to withdraw until she found out why Frances had gone. It might have had no direct bearing on their love, but it certainly had an indirect one.

'I . . . I'm sorry, Dad,' Rory was saying, and Mark wheeled on them both.

'Don't blame yourself, Rory. It wasn't your fault, any of it. I . . . I even deserved to be kept in the dark. I can see that. I . . . I haven't been much of a father, have I?'

'Now stop that,' said Deborah sharply, aware that he was tormenting himself with self-reproach. 'The main thing is to find Frances. We *must* find her now.'

'Yes, we must,' Rory agreed.

'She's the only one who matters.

Have you got Paul's telephone number, Mark?'

He made an effort to pull himself together.

'Yes. Here . . . ' he fumbled in his pocket. 'Mrs Denham wrote it down for me. I . . . I just told her I wanted his advice about something. Didn't want to upset her.'

He handed it to Deborah, who made for the telephone, then Mark turned to Rory.

'The scoundrel,' he said quietly. 'The child was more or less in his care . . . a man old enough to know better. His parents . . . Tom Wright would be ashamed of his son. Just let him wait!'

'Dad!' cried Rory. 'Don't you see? That's why I couldn't tell you. Don't go trying to fight Lionel, or something. You might just get hurt.'

Mark saw the concern on the boy's face, and felt humble. He didn't deserve their love, but it was there just the same.

'I've been able to use other methods

of chastening people who needed it, other than giving them a good hiding,' he said, with a wry smile. 'Though that's what he needs. Don't worry, Rory, I shan't go brawling at my age, and getting myself spread all over the Sunday newspapers. But I *can* deal with a skunk like Lionel Wright. If only Frances would write or telephone. If only young Denham has seen her . . . '

Deborah walked through from the hall a few moments later, shaking her head.

'I got through to Paul's number, but he was out. It was a woman who answered, probably his landlady. She says he'll ring back when he comes in. He's due to take a youth club tonight. Meanwhile, do let's have some tea. It might make us all feel better.'

They had poor appetites, and it was a silent meal, each of them busy with their own thoughts. When the telephone rang, it was Deborah who again went to answer it. They could hear her low attractive voice, though very little of the conversation, then the receiver was replaced.

'Oh dear, now I think Paul is upset and worried, too,' she said, as she returned. 'He hasn't seen her, or heard from her for some time, but he'll ring here as soon as he does. I . . . I told him if anyone else came asking about her, to tell him nothing, and that you'd deal with it, Mark. I hope that was right?'

Mark nodded, his face morose.

'I'll leave first thing in the morning, Deborah. Actually I have business in Manchester, but if Wright goes there to see young Denham, then he is having priority!'

'Let me come, too, Dad,' pleaded Rory.

Mark hesitated, considering.

'All right, Rory, you can come, too. I'll have to ring up Robert McLean at the office. Bob was marvellous at the time of the accident. And since. But obviously it isn't over,' he added, rather bitterly.

'It will be,' Deborah consoled him.

'Don't worry, Mark, it will be. Just as soon as you find Frances.'

There was a certain amount of peace in her heart, now that she realised she and Mark had not been the cause of the young girl running away from home. Now, underneath the worry, there was quiet happiness that she and Mark could be together after all.

But there was no such underlying happiness in Mark. He was still reproaching himself for the anxieties his children had suffered, so that he looked at Deborah almost as a stranger. She was young and lovely, and could do a lot better for herself than a man like himself. He had probably only caught her at an unhappy time in her life, when she was recovering from losing her husband, and finding someone else on whom to depend.

'We'll see,' he said, rather harshly. 'As I say, we'll leave in the morning. I . . . we can discuss things another time.'

Deborah felt her throat beginning to sting with tears. Mark had been upset,

249

but surely he could see that she was there to comfort him, and he could meet her half-way. Was he still hurt and angry because she had put him off till they found Frances? Or had Rory brought back memories of his dead wife, which made him suddenly feel that he didn't really want to put anyone in her place? Would things be changed between them from now on?

The thought made her feel hollow inside, but she had no time for brooding as Amy and her small friend came in from the garden, and she busied herself with getting them both something to eat, and seeing the child safely home.

But Rock House had never seemed so lonely when Mark and Rory left for the airport next morning, not even during the days following Patrick's death. Deborah missed her new family more than she had ever thought possible.

But most of all she missed Mark.

11

Paul Denham put down the telephone, his eyes dark and brooding. For over a week now he'd had an uneasy feeling about Frances. She wasn't a good correspondent, but she never left him longer than two weeks without a note of some kind, scrappy though it might be. He had grown to accept her troubled nature, and he wrote her long letters, feeling he must hold on to the link between them, and she had responded as he hoped she would by replying, sometimes quite quickly, and sometimes keeping him waiting for two long weeks. But never longer than that, he remembered. And this time it was almost three.

Paul had settled down well as curate of a busy city parish, and he was trying to give his heart and soul to the job. If it had not been for Frances, he knew that his every thought and care would have been for his new parishioners, but always she was there, at the back of his mind, even while he went about his duties, and filling his whole mind and heart when he finally closed the door of his room each evening.

There was no curate's house in the parish, as their large old church was too poor and too expensive to allow more than the upkeep of a rambling old vicarage. There the vicar, the Reverend William Davis, lived with his wife and ageing parents, but lodgings had been found for Paul with an elderly couple, Mr and Mrs Bradwell, in a rather nice, spacious suburban house.

Mrs Bradwell had rented Paul two rooms on the first floor, and it was there he found sanctuary, tired out with walking the hard pavements and visiting the many people who needed guidance of one kind or another. Paul's early days had been difficult as he quickly realised how little he knew about the job he had undertaken, and about the people he served. But a quick mind and a good memory had soon been employed to good use, and he was able to be of more practical help. He filled in forms, wrote letters, contacted local authorities, talked to teenagers at the behest of parents, husbands at the behest of wives, and telephoned distant sons and daughters on behalf of elderly, forgotten parents.

In between times he wrote his sermon for Sunday.

'I'm giving you the Youth Club,' William Davis had told him when he first went to the parish. 'It takes a young man like you to understand young people, I think. You'll find quite a number of youngsters helpful and appreciative, glad of the opportunity of forming a club and having fun together. But there's always the destructive element. Watch out for them, Paul. They can undo a lot of good work. And remember, the Church Hall is for the use of the church as a whole, not just the Youth Club. Everything must be tidied away before the Club breaks up in the evening, because the hall will be used by the Over-60's, or the Dancing Club the following evening. It may seem a small point, but it's just these little things which can cause most dissension.'

'I understand,' said Paul.

'Oh, and there are also outside sources of trouble I hope you'll be able to solve. Some young rascals feel it's a lot of fun to come poking in after the Club is under way. They hang round the door, break milk bottles on the step, shout derisive remarks, or just hang around being insolent. I . . . I used to try to get them to join in, and indeed it would be a fine thing if they would consent to . . . well, become one of our members. A fine thing.'

Mr Davis looked out of his study window reflectively, to the long narrow streets, over-populated and busy with traffic. It wasn't easy for young people to work off surplus energy, he thought, without getting into mischief of some kind. But it had grieved him that some young lads would try so hard to spoil things for their own contemporaries. He had tried to reason with them, but had felt powerless against their sneers and catcalls.

He sighed. The closely-built houses could also produce the sort of love for one another which often warmed his heart. That was what made it all worthwhile.

He turned to look at Paul. Maybe he could do better with the hooligans. He looked a strong lad physically as well as spiritually.

'Do your best, my boy,' he said. 'Do your best. That's all I ask. Oh, and don't forget to collect dibs. The cost of the hall is twenty shillings per night . . . heating and light, you know.'

'A pound?'

'That's it. A pound.'

Paul's eyes twinkled. He had learned that Mr Davis was inclined to hop about from the idealistic to the mundane. In fact, Paul found that one of his attractions.

The Youth Club had flourished under his hands, though at first they seemed to have a large number of young ladies wishing to join. Paul, however, was an expert at dealing with such matters, and soon he had the youngsters interested in the Club for its own sake, and a spirit of pride began to make itself felt.

The outside elements had presented more problems, but Paul was still young enough to remember how he had dealt with boys who had been offensive to him at school. With surprise Mr Davis's 'young rascals' found they were no longer dealing with kindly Mr Davis, and found themselves being thrown out rather forcibly.

Paul had later had misgivings, fully expecting to be set upon one quiet evening, but it was with some amusement and a quiet inward gratitude, that he saw his own club members were keeping an eye on him. Instead of seeing them safely on their way, they took to tidying up the room, and waiting while he locked up, then they enjoyed a little talk while walking home together.

It would have been exciting and exhilarating but for Frances. Like it or not, Paul was forced to acknowledge that Frances had a place in his heart that no one had ever held before. He was in love with her, and at first he felt unhappy that she obviously didn't feel the same way. But she had said more in her letters than she had perhaps realised, and gradually he began to feel that it was something else which stood between them, something which was shadowing her life.

And now she had run away from home without telling her father, or Deborah Lacey, where to find her. Not even Rory knew! Yet surely she had sense enough to know that one couldn't run away from problems. One took problems along, and they were only resolved by facing up to them. Giants could be shrunk quite a bit by making a stand. If only she would come to him, thought Paul. He could help her, he was sure, even if it should be at some cost to himself.

His thoughts went again to his conversation with Deborah.

'If anyone else comes asking about her, Mr Nesbit will deal with it, Paul,' she had said.

Who would be asking about Frances? Who would know he and she even *knew* one another, outside their own circle of friends and relatives? Was it someone trying to be helpful when the family wanted to keep the matter in their own hands?

Paul pondered as he walked through the streets to the Church Hall, to prepare for the usual busy noisy evening. There would be dancing and table tennis, snooker and . . . a recent innovation . . . gymnastics, at which he excelled. He was teaching the young men how to control and discipline their bodies, with a view to controlling and disciplining their minds. Success was beginning to come, though one or two were showing off a little, and Paul was keeping a wary eye on them. An accident could often undo quite a lot of good work.

For once the noise rather grated on his nerves, and no doubt his edginess communicated itself to the youngsters because small quarrels broke out, minor irritations normally, but tonight they made Paul long for the peace and quiet of his rooms. If only he could think!

★ ★ ★

Paul was sorting out a quarrel when he saw the tall, well-built man at the door, looking round rather hesitantly. Excusing himself, Paul walked forward.

'Mr Denham?'

'Yes.'

'Sorry to intrude. My name is Lionel Wright and I'm an old friend of the Nesbit family. I . . . I wonder if I might have a word with you.'

His glance indicated the noise which was going on, though he only raised his voice by a tone.

'Of course.'

Paul looked round, then showed his visitor into a small ante-room. He felt curious, but relieved too. From the hasty remarks Deborah had made on the phone, he had been afraid that some boy had become interested in Frances and was making a nuisance of himself, so it was rather a relief to see this older man, who was no doubt a friend of the family. Yet a sense of uncertainty assailed him as he followed Lionel into the room. Could there be something else about Frances about which he didn't know? He curbed the questions which were trembling to be asked, having learned restraint in his profession.

'It isn't awfully salubrious,' he apologised with a quiet smile, 'but at least there's less noise.'

'How can you stand it?' said Lionel Wright.

'It's my job. Now, Mr Wright, how can I help you?'

Lionel's gaze swept over the young man. He had been disconcerted by Paul Denham's appearance. Was this the reason why Frances was so changed towards him? As a young girl she had hung on his every word, and it had pleased him very much. He had felt his power over her, and firmly believed that although she was trying to break free, because of vague connections with the death of her mother, which was really nothing to do with him at all, underneath her feeling for him was only dormant. He could rouse her to even greater love for him, he told himself, with quiet satisfaction. Young girls like Frances needed an older man. A boy of her own age would only bore her.

Yet this Paul Denham seemed a rather mature young man for his age. Then Lionel remembered, again, that he was a priest and he sighed with relief. There would be nothing personal in his relationship with Frances.

He sat down on a rather uncomfortable chair and regarded Paul.

'I believe you know Miss Frances Nesbit,' he said gently.

Paul inclined his head.

'Her people are a trifle . . . er . . . concerned. Frances has been wanting to spread her wings . . . quite usual in a young girl . . . but rather thoughtlessly she hasn't let her father or brother know where she's staying. Not unnaturally they're concerned, and as I was coming over to the mainland, I . . . well, I thought I would try to find her. Mrs Lacey . . . the housekeeper, you know . . . remembered that she had made you her confidante. We wondered if she'd been in touch?'

Lionel's eyebrows rose and Paul continued to regard him steadily. He was an odd man, he thought, yet no doubt Mark Nesbit found him dependable.

'You're an old friend from Glasgow?' he enquired.

'Yes.'

'You've known Frances a long time?'

Lionel frowned. There was no need

for an inquisition.

'A very long time. I assure you, I *am* an old friend.'

'Of course.' Paul still hesitated, trying to fathom Lionel. 'I'm sorry,' he said at length. 'I haven't seen Frances for at least two months. Not since I left the island to come to this parish.'

'Oh.' The man's disappointment was obvious. 'If she should come to ask your advice, could you give me a ring? Only please don't mention anything about me to Frances. That's important. Her . . . her father is anxious about her and wants to see her settled, but . . . well, she's a headstrong girl. If she thinks you're going to inform her family, she might disappear again very quickly. You understand?'

'I understand.'

Paul made no promise as he took the telephone number. He would certainly want to do some checking up before seeing Lionel Wright again. There was gnawing anxiety in his own heart about Frances, and he understood how the

Nesbits felt, but he wondered about this smooth man who was an old family friend. Now that he'd had time for reflection, perhaps it was this man whom Deborah Lacey had warned him against on the phone.

But why? What harm could he do to Frances?

As Paul showed his visitor out, he looked at the business card, with the name and number of the hotel where Lionel was staying written on the back, and put it carefully in his pocket. There was no harm in knowing where Mr Wright could be found.

Then Paul returned to the mêlée which was the Youth Club, and his anxiety lent him an impatience not normal to his nature, so that several of his members found themselves brought up sharply, and obeying quick instructions when they'd had no intentions of doing anything other than make mischief. The curate didn't stand any nonsense.

Nevertheless Paul was tired as he

made his way home, locking up after the youngsters had gone. As he turned away, a figure detached itself from the shadows and ran to him in the darkness.

'Paul?'

He whirled, his heart missing a beat, then racing like mad.

'Frances?'

She was in his arms, being held as though he would never let her go, and one or two of the Youth Club members, who had hung about to see Mr Denham home, were electrified to see that their curate was just an ordinary young man after all, slightly older than themselves. Though it was quite a shock to find that he was human. With interest they watched him prove it, then they melted away quickly. Who'd have thought it? Mr Denham! With a girl!

'Where are you staying, darling? You must come home with me first of all,' said Paul, urgently.

Frances was trembling like a leaf.

'Oh, Paul, I'm so frightened. He . . . he was here, wasn't he? Lionel?'

'Mr Wright? Yes. Why, you aren't afraid of him, are you? What need is there to be afraid of him?'

'Oh, Paul, it's a long story, and I'm so tired. Only I *am* afraid of him. I can't tell you now. I don't want him to find me, even to see me. I've got to hide somewhere . . . '

'For goodness' sake!' cried Paul, then caught back his words. Frances was worn out. All explanations could keep. 'Come on, darling,' he said gently. 'Home to my digs. There's a spare room and I'm sure you can have it. The Bradwells won't turn you away. Bed for you, then you can tell me all about it in the morning.'

Frances sighed. It seemed to her that for the first time in two years, her heart was at rest. Paul would take care of everything.

Mrs Bradwell couldn't conceal her surprise when her young curate lodger turned up in the late evening, with a very pretty girl who was introduced as his fiancée.

'Miss Nesbit has been rather unwell,' he explained, 'and upset over something, so she decided to come and see me. Miss Nesbit lives next door to my parents in the Isle of Man.'

Mrs Bradwell thought it rather strange that she hadn't heard about Miss Nesbit before now, but there was no doubt the clergy were reticent about such things. And in any case, the poor girl looked dead on her feet.

She had always kept the two attic bedrooms for use since her daughter took up nursing. One never knew the minute when Sandra would arrive home with another nurse in tow. Now it was an easy matter to prepare the bedroom for Miss Nesbit.

Frances felt as though she were drowning in luxury as she slipped between the sheets, warmed up by an electric blanket. She managed to drink the hot malted milk Mrs Bradwell provided, then she fell asleep, too exhausted to worry any more.

It was a different story next morning, however, when she woke up and realisation returned. She was in a strange house ... Paul's lodgings ... being acknowledged as his fiancée! For a short while she lay savouring the feeling of security it gave her, then she threw back the covers and leapt out of bed. It was all wrong. She couldn't allow Paul to protect her like this. She would have to leave again. It wasn't fair to him.

Softly she tiptoed downstairs, just as Mrs Bradwell came out of Paul's sitting-room and beamed on her.

'We've been letting you sleep, my dear. You were very tired. I was just going to come up with a tray, but you can have your breakfast downstairs now.'

'I'm not hungry,' said Frances quickly.

'If you could eat it, a good breakfast would put new strength into you. Mr Denham had to go over to the church, but he'll be back in a moment. He'll want a bit, too. He does an eight o'clock Communion this morning.'

'Oh.'

Frances felt trapped. She could hardly rush downstairs and bolt away, yet she didn't want to stay and face Paul either. Maybe he was regretting, now, that she had foisted herself on to him, yet he had been wonderful to her. He had made her feel wanted. He cared for her, and that would always warm her heart, but she would be no good in his life.

Then suddenly he was there, in the hall, a shaft of sunlight on his hair, just as she had seen him that morning sitting at the cove. Her heart seemed to lurch, then to race, as he hurried forward and held out his arms. Mrs Bradwell looked on for a moment, indulgently, then hurried into the kitchen. There was no doubt it was a love match, she thought contentedly.

'We must talk, Paul,' Frances told him. 'I can't let you . . . '

'What? Don't try to pretend you don't love me as I love you? I knew as soon as I saw you again that we belong together, and I shan't let you go again, Frances. If you're in trouble, I want to hear all about it. I have that right. And I want to know why you're scared of that chap, Wright.'

'All right, Paul,' she agreed. 'I'll tell you everything. Can we go somewhere and talk?'

'I have a sitting-room. But first of all, we eat Mrs Bradwell's excellent breakfast.'

After a while it was easy to tell Paul all about Lionel Wright, and apart from the grim lines which suddenly appeared round his mouth, he gave no sign of his feelings till Frances had finished. She pushed back the hair from her flushed face, and looked at him, her eyes dark with forcing back the tears.

'So you see, Paul, why I . . . I just couldn't allow us to . . . to be more than friends. Not even that, at first. I mean, you're a curate and I . . . I've always felt responsible for Mother . . . '

She was in tears, being held tightly against him while he soothed her, and stroked her dark hair.

'A good cry will get it out of you, darling, but I've never heard such rubbish, taking all the blame on yourself,' said Paul roundly, 'and to think that Rory encouraged you . . . '

'He didn't!'

'He should have shown more common sense. Both of you making cases out of yourselves with worry, when a word to your father could have put it all right.'

'Oh, I couldn't tell Daddy!'

Paul kissed her.

'What sort of man do you think he is? Anyway, he probably knows by now. If you haven't kept Rory informed, he'll be too worried about you to keep his mouth shut. But this . . . this hound . . . '

'Lionel. Oh, Paul, when I saw you talking to him and remembered that I'd once thought he was so handsome

. . . once thought I loved him . . . I felt so ashamed. You and he. You can't know what I feel.'

Paul's face had gone white again, his anger against Lionel Wright a hard knot inside him.

'Leave him to me,' he said quietly.

Deborah Lacey *had* warned him, but he could never have guessed all this. It was incongruous.

'But he won't go away. I know he won't. I've tried to make him, and he always just agrees, but I can't make him see, so he just comes back again.'

'Like a handful of mist, as you describe it,' said Paul. 'Well, I know one thing guaranteed to disperse the mist, and that's sunshine. So cheer up, darling, and let's have some happiness instead. I promise you that Lionel Wright will never bother you again. We're getting married, and you can put the past behind you where it belongs.'

'But if people knew how . . . how silly I've been. Your parishioners . . . '

'Make far bigger mistakes, and in

272

many cases, it doesn't worry them in the least. That makes a much bigger problem. No, Frances, in some ways times have changed for the better. Besides, don't you think that if you've had worries and troubles of your own, then you'll be much more sympathetic towards those who need our help?'

For a moment Paul looked at Frances, his eyes concerned.

'In fact, I'm being selfish in asking you to share my life. It isn't going to be easy. We'll probably be hard up most of the time, and you won't believe the number of problems that arise. Maybe you should think again.'

This time the sun shone from Frances' face, and he saw that unwittingly he had struck the right note.

'Oh, Paul, of course none of that will matter. Oh, if only you knew what it feels like to come in out of the darkness!'

Again there was a glint in his eyes, however, as he silently remembered the name of the hotel where Lionel

Wright was staying. This morning he intended to keep a very important date there!

'Now, darling, I have work to do, but I want you to stay here for a day or two till we make plans. First things first, though. You must ring up your father and Deborah Lacey, because they've been very worried about you. Tell them you're safe and tell them our news. I'll have to talk to your father, of course . . .'

Paul's eyes darkened again. He hoped Mark Nesbit would find him a suitable son-in-law.

'That's enough,' said Frances, her eyes amused. She was beginning to read Paul very well.

'All right,' he laughed. 'I'll be free for an hour this afternoon. I'll take you to meet the rector, Mr Davis, then we'll buy the ring.'

'I shall insist on a whopping great diamond,' said Frances mischievously.

'You'll be lucky not to have one out of Woolworth's. I must ring home, too

. . . before Mrs Lacey says anything to Mother!'

'Oh, goodness! I forgot! What if she doesn't like me?'

Paul laughed.

'Maybe she won't, and maybe you won't like her. But I think you will love one another dearly. Anyway, you aren't marrying her, darling. You're marrying me.'

Frances nodded, then went to the window to look out on the solid streets of Manchester. It wasn't exactly the view from her bedroom window on the island, but at the moment it was the loveliest place in the world. She could see shady trees and brilliant flowers in neat gardens. Bright windows looked fresh with colourful curtains, and the hum of the traffic was like a heartbeat. And soon it would be her home.

12

It was a week later before Frances saw the island again. The Reverend William Davis had beamed approval on her and offered Paul a week's leave, so that they could both go back home and arrange an engagement party.

'I'm very pleased, my dear,' he told Frances, after he had assured himself that she was not a 'silly girl'. 'Do the job properly, though. It's a long while since my wife and I held an engagement party, but we did the job properly.'

That evening Mark and Rory turned up looking for Paul, and found Frances instead, moving rather restlessly in Paul's sitting-room. He had gone out on business, but she had a shrewd suspicion as to what the business might be.

That afternoon she had phoned home to Deborah, and learned that her father and Rory were on their way to Manchester.

'I'm sorry, Frances. I could only think of Paul Denham. I knew you and he were friends . . . '

Deborah's voice sounded strange, but it might have been a bad line.

'I'm the one to be sorry,' said Frances ruefully. 'I shouldn't have run away. I know that now. Sorry you were worried, Deb . . . '

'I'm just relieved to hear from you now, Frances.'

This time the voice was clearer.

'Paul and I have news for you,' Frances told her. 'We're engaged.'

There was a short silence.

'I'm very happy for you both.'

'We'll tell Daddy when he comes. And Rory.'

'Yes.'

Again there was that faint hesitation and Frances put down the telephone after Deborah had rung off. Was Debbie angry with her? She couldn't blame her, but she felt rather depressed at losing even a part of the regard she had thought Deborah felt for her. She really cared for the older woman, and suddenly wanted to see her again.

When Paul left her at his lodgings, she felt restless and unsettled, then her father and Rory had arrived, and Frances stared at them both for a long moment, then ran to her father, the tears again in her eyes.

'Oh, Daddy, I'm so sorry. I . . . I expect Rory has told you . . . '

'Yes. Have you seen Wright since you left home?'

Frances' cheeks coloured furiously.

'I feel so ashamed. He . . . he's been here, to see Paul, and now I think Paul has called on him at his hotel. He said he would . . . would send him away. Paul and I are engaged.'

'Well, at least you've got some sense in you,' said Rory.

'Which hotel?' Mark was asking. 'I want a word with him, too.'

'I don't know. Paul wouldn't tell me.'

Later, when Paul came home, he and

278

Mark had a few quiet words together.

'He won't ever bother Frances again,' said Paul quietly.

'I want to see him,' Mark said.

'I rather think he'll be on his way back to London. But I left him in no doubt how you felt . . . how we all felt. As I say, we've seen the last of him. Oh, and Mr Nesbit . . . I would like to marry Frances.'

Mark's eyes crinkled.

'I think that would please us all.'

Nevertheless, he *still* had a date with Lionel Wright!

★ ★ ★

It seemed strange to have her family all back home again, thought Deborah, and this time they *were* all her family. Mark had telephoned from Manchester, a new note of happiness in his voice, and somehow everything had come right again between them.

Deborah had asked him to delay their own plans, however, so that Frances could have her full happiness.

'We've had it all before, Mark,' she insisted. 'We're older, and can wait.'

'Speak for yourself,' he grinned.

He and Rory had gone back to Glasgow, and now it was arranged that Rory should start work in the firm.

'It will mean living in Glasgow,' Mark told Deborah. 'I feel that I must give more time again to the business. Robert McLean has been shouldering a bigger load than he should over the past few months, though there was a time when I did that for him. That's the way it goes.'

'I shan't mind,' Deborah told him.

'We'll find a housekeeper for this house, and come back as often as we can. Will Amy settle in Glasgow?'

'Amy's adaptable. So long as she has our love, she'll settle anywhere.'

Mark paused, hesitantly.

'We can look for another house, darling. I shan't ask you to live in our present one.'

Deborah shook her head.

'No, we won't, Mark. Not if you like

it. It was your old family home after all, and I shan't be seeing Una's ghost flitting everywhere. Or if I do, then she'll be welcome. I think we can both look back on our previous marriages and be grateful for them.'

Mark felt even more grateful for Deborah, and she, too, was content. She remembered the moment when Frances had walked back in the door, and knew that the last of her fears had been allayed.

'Rory told me,' Frances had said simply. 'I'm so glad.'

* * *

Rory took longest to say a temporary goodbye to the island he had grown to love. Some day, if he worked hard at his writing, he might even come back to make his home here.

He called on June to let her know his plans.

'Come for a walk, if your new boy-friend can spare you,' he invited. 'I guess I won't be seeing much of you from now on. I'm going to work, you see, though I'll keep on writing in my spare time.'

'Good for you,' said June, a trifle croakingly, as she cleared her throat. The sun and sea air had again bleached her hair almost white, and turned her skin golden brown.

'He's a lucky chap,' said Rory, thinking for the hundredth time that she looked like a goddess.

'Who?'

'Michael Derby.' He sighed. 'Maybe, when my scar fades a bit, I might find someone, too.'

'Such rubbish! As if that old scar mattered. I wouldn't have cared a bit if . . . '

'We'd fallen in love?'

'Yes.'

'But . . . ' Rory looked at her sideways. 'We didn't, did we?'

'Oh, Rory, you are a fool,' said June. 'Can't you even kiss me goodbye?'

Rory did.

'Who is Mike Derby?' asked June.

Jane Carrick is a pseudonym
of Mary Cummins
who also writes as
Mary Jane Warmington

We do hope that you have enjoyed reading this large print book.

Did you know that all of our titles are available for purchase?

We publish a wide range of high quality large print books including:
Romances, Mysteries, Classics
General Fiction
Non Fiction and Westerns

Special interest titles available in large print are:
The Little Oxford Dictionary
Music Book, Song Book
Hymn Book, Service Book

Also available from us courtesy of Oxford University Press:
Young Readers' Dictionary
(large print edition)
Young Readers' Thesaurus
(large print edition)

For further information or a free brochure, please contact us at:
Ulverscroft Large Print Books Ltd.,
The Green, Bradgate Road, Anstey,
Leicester, LE7 7FU, England.
Tel: (00 44) **0116 236 4325**
Fax: (00 44) **0116 234 0205**

VISIONS OF THE HEART

Christine Briscomb

When property developer Connor Grant contracted Natalie Jensen to landscape the grounds of his large country house near Ashley in South Australia, she was ecstatic. But then she discovered he was acquiring — and ripping apart — great swathes of the town. Her own mother's house and the hall where the drama group met were two of his targets. Natalie was desperate to stop Connor's plans — but she also had to fight the powerful attraction flowing between them.

DIVIDED LOYALTIES

Phyllis Demaine

When Heather's fiancé, Adrian, is offered a wonderful job in America their future seems rosy. However, Adrian's brother, Carl, a widower, asks for Heather's help with his small, deaf son. Help which, as a speech therapist, Heather is qualified to give. But things become complicated when Carl goes abroad on business and returns with Gisel, to whom his son takes an instant dislike. This puts Heather in the position of having to choose between the boy's happiness and her own.

THE PERFECT GENTLEMAN

Liz Pedersen

When Laura agrees to help Anthony Christopher to deceive his family she has no idea how far the web of intrigue will extend, or how it will alter her life. His family is as unpleasant as he promised, but Laura drives away from his funeral thinking she has escaped their malicious clutches. However, this is not so. James Christopher is determined to discover what was behind his cousin's precipitate marriage. He despises Laura and hates the fact that he is attracted to her.

FINGALA, MAID OF RATHAY

Mary Cummins

On his deathbed, Sir James Mont-
gomery of Rathay asks his daughter,
Fingala, to swear that she will not
honour her marriage contract until
her brother Patrick, the new heir,
returns from serving the King.
Patrick must marry. Rathay must
not be left without a mistress. But
Patrick has fallen in love with the
Lady Catherine Gordon whom the
King, James IV, has given in
marriage to the young man who
claims to be Richard of York, one of
the princes in the Tower.

ZABILLET OF THE SNOW

Catherine Darby

For Zabillet, a young peasant girl growing up in the tiny French village of Fromage in the mid-fourteenth century, a respectable marriage is the height of her parents' ambitions for her. But life is changing. Zabillet's love for a handsome shepherd is tested when she is invited to join the La Neige household, where her mistress, Lady Petronella, has plans for her grandson, Benet. And over all broods the horror of the Great Death that claims all whom it touches.

PERILOUS JOURNEY

Caroline Joyce

After the execution of Charles I, Louisa's Royalist father considers it too dangerous for her to stay in England and arranges for her to go to the Isle of Man with Armand de la Tremouille, the nephew of the island's Royalist Governor. Their ship is boarded by Parliamentarians who plan to sail for Ireland, but a storm causes them to be shipwrecked on the Calf of Man. Magnus Stapleton, the Parliamentarian chief, becomes infatuated with Louisa, but she has fallen in love with Armand.